MERC

THE BLUE-EYED BOY

MERCENARY 10

THE BLUE-EYED BOY

Richard McLaughlin

First published in Great Britain 1995
22 Books, Invicta House, Sir Thomas Longley Road,
Rochester, Kent

Copyright © 1995 by 22 Books

The moral right of the author has been asserted

A CIP catalogue record for this book is available from the
British Library

ISBN 1 898125 44 9

10 9 8 7 6 5 4 3 2 1

Typeset by Hewer Text Composition Services, Edinburgh
Printed in Great Britain by Cox and Wyman Limited, Reading

1

The phone rang. Carlisle's eyes opened. They looked like those of a cat startled by the headlights of a car. It was one-thirty. He lifted the receiver; there was nothing but a dull hum.

'Hello?' said Carlisle. Still nothing. 'Hello?' He felt his wife stir, and looked over his shoulder. A wide band of moonlight lay across Kate's half-uncovered body. He felt a wave of tenderness and then anger. 'OK then, I'll tell you what: you give me your name, rank and number and I'll tell you where to stick your pervy . . .'

'I'm afraid I can't help you with the former, Carlisle, but then, as I'm sure you'll appreciate, I have my reasons.'

Carlisle froze. He knew the voice. 'What the bloody hell do you want?' he said. Another silence: ten, maybe twelve, seconds. Carlisle watched the second hand of the bedside clock. Each tick banged like a steam hammer in his head and with each blow he became more aware that for the second time in his life he was beginning to panic.

'Listen, I can't, I . . . it's better we don't speak here. Have you got the other number? The one I . . .'

The voice cut him short with an immediate answer. 'It's 0171–372–6907, isn't it?'

'Christ Almighty, what sort of machine am I talking to here?'

'Quite an efficient one. Shall we say ten minutes?'

'Do I have a choice?'

No answer.

'Ten minutes it is, then,' said Carlisle.

The number Carlisle had given was that of a public phone box near his flat in north London. He dressed, and within a minute was walking through what he thought for a moment was a fine drizzle. Then he realized his clothes were soaked in sweat.

He picked up the receiver on the second ring.

'Carlisle?' The voice sounded as dead as before.

'No, Shirley Temple, and this is the Good Ship Lollipop.'

After a silence the voice repeated mechanically, 'Carlisle?'

'What, for fuck's sake?'

'Is there anyone with or near you?'

Carlisle looked down the road. It was as empty as roads can only be in the early hours. 'It's nearly two in the morning. What the fuck do you think?'

'I repeat, is there anyone with or near . . .?'

'No!'

'Good, then listen closely. There is a parcel for you to collect. You need to be at the Park Lane end of Mount Street. Walk down to where South Audley Street crosses . . .'

'By Purdey's the gunmakers'?'

'. . . To where South Audley Street crosses it, and turn right. Walk fifty yards and turn left. On your left is a small public library. Ahead of you are the gates to a public garden. Walk through those gates at precisely 7.20 this morning, 8 June. You'll see a man seated on the third bench; he'll stand and turn as you enter the garden. He will have left a parcel for you to collect. Is that clear?'

'I thought there weren't going to be any more parcels to collect.'

'I'm not able to comment, I'm afraid. But I must ask you again: is everything clear?'

'Yes,' said Carlisle, and then, as he replaced the receiver, he said aloud to himself, 'What the hell sort of machine am I talking to here?'

He looked to his right. The high Victorian buildings formed a sort of canyon down which the breeze carried the debris of the night's pleasures. A bag snagged on what he'd thought was a pile of rubbish. The pile moved; it was a drunk. Carlisle walked over and looked down at the man, who stared up at him. His skin was dark red in places, almost like a Victoria plum. His unblinking eyes were pure dazzling blue. They looked new, like a baby's. Carlisle reached inside his blazer for his wallet. He took from it

3

a £50 note and placed it in the drunk's claw-like hand. The man stuffed it into a pocket and rolled over. Carlisle knew then that he would never know why he had done that.

Back home, he crept into the bedroom. The band of moonlight had moved further down Kate's body and divided it just above her bottom. He wanted to dive into that moonlit corridor and be consumed and never return. Instead he turned and walked softly away.

Carlisle closed the door to his study and slipped a CD into the player. He took a glass and a nearly full bottle of Bushmills from the cabinet and sank into his armchair. He poured a glass as the first bars of the adagio from Beethoven's Seventh Symphony filled the headphones. Beethoven and Bushmills. Not bad mates when you're in a spot. The first mouthful of malt rinsed over his gums, burning and scouring. He liked the pain. With one gulp he sent the malt down to his stomach. More burning, more pain – as if he'd been speared in the guts.

Eleven years earlier things had looked so different. After the Falklands inquiry it was considered appropriate that he should leave the Parachute Regiment 'quietly' and that no more would be said. With a major's pension and some decent contacts, things looked OK. He'd been offered a partnership in a set-up that trained Outward Bound managers. Then he'd met his partner's daughter, Kate, fallen in love and married her. From then on, as far as he was concerned, ex-Major Peter Carlisle, 3 Para, was in the pink.

In 1985 he got the first phone call. Just a voice. Someone – he had no idea who – so far up the chain of command you'd need a radio telescope to see him. Carlisle was familiar with terms like 'irregular activities' and 'CE' (classified exceptional). It all sounded a bit like cowboys and Indians. A lark, really, and so much dosh you could eat, drink and wipe your arse on the stuff and still have the bus fare home. But it wasn't a lark and it couldn't go on like this. Kate was no fool. Sooner or later she'd rumble his lies. She'd probably rumbled them already. One day he would come back and find that all the king's horses and all the king's men just couldn't put Peter together again. They'd only just managed last time.

When he thought of that last time he shuddered like some kid being hit by his first slug of whisky. It was Iran, '91. A 'sleeper' had to be got out. Half-Turkish, half-Iranian, he operated under cover, as a dealer in rare timbers. After five years in the land of the mullahs he'd cracked the IDs of some particularly elusive arms dealers, only to be rumbled by his young servant with whom he had a more than cordial understanding.

Clued up that his boss was moving out, the youth thought he'd help himself to a little plunder while he still could. Sex, meat and sleep had been their usual evening routine and while the boss was indulging in the latter his hitherto faithful lover-cum-servant made off with the most valuable-looking item in the house: a security briefcase whose contents would have put two high-ranking UN officials, a German MP and a French cabinet minister in prison for a well-earned rest. They had all been busy boys.

Carlisle and his cavalry had been sent to pull out the sleeper, or what was left of him, and maybe take a scalp or two on the way. The plan was Carlisle's and had variously been called audacious, mad and suicidal. But it had worked. Almost.

Carlisle was acting as decoy on a remote border road with Turkey. He was within nine miles of the border when a flash-flood ripped up the road and barred his exit to freedom. He wired up the vehicle and simulated a fatal accident, but it fooled no one. Before nightfall they had him. Two hours later, on the orders of their holiest of holy men, Iranian torturers were plying their most ancient of trades.

He would never know how much more he could have taken. His jaw had been smashed and half of his teeth had gone, along with the fingernails of his left hand. Then they sent a medic in. He looked European and had a fatherly, almost concerned, look. He sat by Carlisle and gave him a drink of water, which he took in painful swallows. Then the medic spoke. 'It's best you tell them everything. There are far less pleasant ways than this.'

'Is that right? Just you go ahead and try them.'

'I'm quite serious. What you are suffering now is uncivilized. It is inhuman. But at least it will end.'

'You think so? I'm pleased to hear that.'

'Please listen. I'm serious. It will end. Even if they torture you for fifty years it will end. But they have things here, drugs, I have seen them used on Kurds. Are you listening to me?'

'Yeah, but you're getting nowhere.'

'You must try to understand. These Kurds, they are devout men. Their beliefs are simple. Beyond death awaits paradise. They would endure anything, anything on earth for that prize and yet . . .'

'Look, if you've been sent in to soften me up then forget it, OK?'

The medic was silent. He stared at Carlisle the way lovers stare at disappearing trains. He spoke slowly and clearly to Carlisle for the last time.

'Mr Carlisle, I have seen these men, devout men, beg for death. Please, Mr Carlisle.'

Back in England, after the usual covert exchanges had been completed they got him to a detox unit where his screams were so bad the ward had to be soundproofed. Six weeks later Kate was allowed to see him. She was so shocked she miscarried. It would have been their first child.

By the time Carlisle had reached the end of these thoughts there was a merciful amount of Bushmills swimming in his brain. He took off the headphones, walked over to the cabinet with calm resolution, pulled open the seventh drawer and took his Browning automatic from its usual place. He checked the working parts, then unlocked the lower drawer of his desk and took two rounds from their box. He slotted one round home, left the next chamber empty and then slid in the second one. He twirled all six chambers with an expert thumb and placed the gun carefully on his desk. He wrote a brief but passionate note to Kate, then sat down again and listened entranced as the symphony soared to its mighty climax. Timpani and brass were locked together in a vast death struggle as he placed the gun's barrel against the roof of his mouth. It seemed almost to be someone else's finger that squeezed the trigger.

The hammer smashed against an empty chamber and the room went completely quiet. If there were gods of guns and war then they had spared him this time. He had to give thanks for that at least. And he did by draining the last of the malt. Then he slept in the armchair. As he slipped into dreams, his last thought was of the pleading of the medic and those terrible words, 'I have seen them beg for death.'

It was one of those sleeps. The eyelids touch, then open, and that's it. Carlisle felt like something that had been stuffed down the back of the sofa for a year or two. He showered and dressed, then put a final buff on an already polished pair of black brogues. By seven he was in a cab heading down the Edgware Road.

As they approached the Marylebone flyover, the cabby said, 'I don't know how they manage that, it's a busy road this, you know.'

On the flyover someone had printed in red, three-foot capitals: 'Out with rich Tory scum – Workers Revolutionary Party.'

'They lean over the top there and paint it upside down,' said Carlisle. 'It's easy if that's the way you see the world.'

'Clever though,' said the cabby.

Carlisle didn't answer. His mind had flashed back to Mount Longdon in the Falklands. The butchered corpses of twelve young men, all from 3 Para. And all of them the sons of working men and women. Maybe they had missed the revolution.

Mount Street was where it usually was and so was everything else. He passed the library and at the moment he entered the garden an anonymous figure on his right rose, looked briefly at him, then walked at a steady pace away to the south gate. 'Anonymity must be an art,' he thought as he looked down at the buff A4 envelope that had been left for him.

The garden was a beautiful place. Well-tended flower-beds were being doused by sprinklers. The lawns were cut trim and mature oaks and beeches gave welcome shade on hot days. A party of schoolchildren came in by the west gate. They were no more than seven or eight years old. Boys and girls, they all wore light-blue and grey uniforms and each held another's hand as they passed in an old-fashioned crocodile through the garden. They stopped briefly by a mellow brick wall to be counted, as Carlisle began opening the envelope. From an open window above them a soft, clear voice trilled out 'Sweet Lass of Richmond Hill'. Some of the children giggled and a blonde girl whispered to her friend, then kissed her on the cheek.

They were still giggling as Carlisle studied the top sheet from the envelope. It was a ten by eight black and white photo of an obscenely mutilated corpse. Both eyes had been cut out and both ears removed, along with the genitals. The feet and hands had been crushed. On the reverse of the print it said in pencil: 'One of ours. Locate and reciprocate.'

There were a few pages of technical data, maps and notes, then another grisly photo. A corpse was hanging from a thick branch of a tree, to the trunk of which was nailed a red flag bearing two black eagles. There were two deep gashes where the man's eyes should have been. An image of 'readers' wives' flashed ludicrously across Carlisle's mind. He felt angry with himself, ashamed of such stupid thoughts. This man had died a terrible death. He'd been disembowelled. When he turned the photo over he felt more than anger. There was a scrawled note, again in pencil: 'One of ours, supposed ID Major Michael Greenwood, ex 3 Para. Suspect: Khodja. Nationality: Albanian.'

Maybe he'd known, maybe not, but the author of that note had signed the death warrant of the man Khodja, whoever he was. For Mike Greenwood had been Carlisle's last remaining close friend. They'd been on Mount Longdon together. As his tears splashed down on the photograph, part of Carlisle died. The part called pity.

2

As usual, Carlisle followed orders. He took all essential contact data and coded it, then destroyed the contents of the envelope. The last thing he dumped in the incinerator in his back garden was the picture of his dear dead friend. As the flames tore through it, the photo rippled and twisted, as though mimicking the agony of the scene it showed.

The next part of the job was going to be the worst. Carlisle's orders were to contact a man called Garvan. His role was described as 'recruiting sergeant', though the nearest this 'sergeant' had been to army action was shooting a popgun at Battersea Fun Fair. As usual, Garvan's overfamiliar manner on the phone made Carlisle feel like throwing up. The two men loathed each other and for his part Carlisle did little to hide the fact. They arranged to meet at Garvan's office the next day.

His office was in Tooley Street, near London Bridge. It was above an import-export business and had no plate. Garvan ushered Carlisle in and shoved his podgy white hand at him.

'Marvellous to see you, Carlisle, and very spruce you're looking too, if I might say so.'

'No law against it,' Carlisle replied.

Garvan chuckled lamely. 'Always to the point, you military chaps,' he said, then began to look through the papers in front of him. A few seconds later he looked up and said with the false bonhomie that Carlisle detested, 'Well, as you've no doubt worked out, Mr Carlisle, we've got a spot of bother down in the Land of the Eagles.'

'You mean Albania?'

'Quite so. Well, it seems that our Albanian cousins are up to a little mischief. Mainly drugs. But the sums are so large it would only take a number of them to team up and they could buy the whole country lock, stock and barrel. And that really wouldn't do, would it?'

'Are they likely to team up?'

'That's for you to find out, old chap. But if your investigations should suggest they are, then . . .'

'Take them out?'

'Good heavens!' squealed Garvan, his hands fluttering in front of him like two flabby little angels. 'I couldn't possibly suggest such a thing. That would be breaking the law. No, no, no, Her Majesty's Government would merely require that you take appropriate steps. Am I making myself clear, Mr Carlisle?'

'Perfectly.'

'Good, then let's find a few comrades-in-arms for you to take along with you, shall we?'

Garvan emptied a large padded envelope on to his desk. The contents were records and photos of men well known to Carlisle. They were all former members of 3 Para and had fought alongside him on Mount Longdon.

'I expect you're familiar with some of these chaps.'

Carlisle nodded.

'Well then, take your pick.'

'What makes you so sure they'll play ball?'

'Well, as you know, we take a keen interest in the activities of certain ex . . .'

'You mean you spy on them,' growled Carlisle.

Garvan continued as though nothing had been said. '. . . and most of the chaps there' – he nodded at the pile of documents – 'will have reason to "join up" again. Five or six anyway. A sort of dirty half-dozen.'

Garvan sniggered at his little joke and placed a cigarette in a holder. He lit it and puffed a plume of smoke lazily in the air.

'Who's this?' Carlisle asked, showing Garvan a photo of a gaunt-looking, dark-haired man in his mid-thirties.

'Interesting chap. Thomas Lane. Was a corporal in the SAS. Found education and was up at Oxford studying law. Came home one night to find his wife had been raped and murdered by what turned out to be drug-pushers. Pretty thing she was too. Now ex-Corporal Lane is in the process of drinking himself to death. If nothing else he should make good CF.'

'CF?'

'Thought you chaps were all jargon. CF. You know, cannon fodder.'

There was an ominous silence. Carlisle could no longer hide his hatred for Garvan and the man knew it.

'Calm down, old chap. It's history,' Garvan went on casually. 'The Romans had their slaves, the Russians had their Tartars. For God's sake, someone's got to be cannon fodder.'

'As long as that someone isn't you. Am I right, you fucking nonce?' Carlisle growled.

'Quite,' said Garvan, who leaned back in his chair and grinned sheepishly at Carlisle.

Now was the wrong time but as Carlisle left the building he vowed to himself that one day he would teach the little shit a lesson he'd never forget.

Back in the car he leafed through the file until he reached the name of Lance-Corporal Richard Hardy. The address was 27 Gloucester Street, Newcastle. Hardy was well named. Back on Mount Longdon after thirty continuous hours of combat, he'd carried a wounded Para half a mile up the mountain to a safe advance stage. He'd been one of Carlisle's best men.

Carlisle drove across London and joined the north-bound throng of traffic on the A1.

Gloucester Street turned out to be on the edge of a shabby council estate close to Newcastle United's ground. Nearly every house had at least one smashed window and the garden wall of number twenty-seven had been flattened. 'Homes fit for heroes,' muttered Carlisle as he rapped loudly on the front door.

'Who is it?' The voice was surly.

Carlisle lifted the flap of the letter-box and called in. 'Hardy, it's Carlisle. Peter Carlisle.'

Hardy opened the front door and gazed at his ex-major.

'What the hell are you doing here, sir?'

'Got a little job for you, Hardy. Heard of a place called Albania?'

'I've heard of it, sir,' said Hardy, looking even more bemused.

'Good, we're going to blow half of it up. Interested?'

Carlisle turned before Hardy had a chance to respond. He went to his car and returned with a full bottle of Bushmills, which he held up for Hardy's inspection. 'Well?'

'You talked me into it, sir.'

'Thought you'd be a hard bastard to crack,' said Carlisle.

As they walked through to Hardy's living room he added, 'Oh, and it's not "sir" any more. It's "Peter" from now on.'

Hardy's flat was spartan in the extreme, and pervaded by the smell of sweaty training gear. They sank a glass in silence, then Carlisle asked, 'So how are things, Rich?'

'So so, you know. It's not a bad life on the dole.

As long as you don't mind giving up luxuries like food and things like that.' Hardy laughed but Carlisle looked sombre.

'You know if I could have done anything – I mean anything.'

'Heads had to role after Longdon. Even I knew that.'

'Maybe, but yours shouldn't have been one of them.'

'Whose then?'

'Good question. Let's just say . . .' Carlisle toyed with his glass and his eyes wandered round the bare room. 'That bayonet on your mantelpiece there – is that the one I think it is?'

'It's one of six, if that's what you mean.'

'One of six they pulled out of Harrison. And how many Argentinian heads rolled for that little atrocity?'

'I take your point,' said Hardy.

Hardy went silent. Before he was tempted to fill the glass with his own tears Carlisle leant across and reached for the Bushmills.

'War is war, old son. And that's that.' Then he lifted his glass. 'To Albania.'

'To Albania,' echoed Hardy.

3

Hardy collected his things and loaded them into Carlisle's car. Within twenty minutes, and still enjoying the warm glow of the Bushmills they were heading down the A1.

'Why Albania?' asked Hardy.

'Drugs – mountains of them. But that's not the real problem. It seems that the families running the trade are getting too rich and too powerful for comfort. There are reports of private armies.'

'Why should that worry us?'

'It's a sensitive part of the world. There's more than enough cowboys running so-called governments in that neck of the woods. I guess Albania would be one too many.'

'And who're they?'

'Let's just say they're the people who'll be paying you five grand a week and they wear white hats.'

'Like the Westerns.'

'In some ways more like the Westerns than you'd ever imagine.' Carlisle paused, then added, 'And in other ways, well, let's just say things can get very rough indeed. There's no cavalry on these jobs. I'll say it now: we won't all be coming back.'

'Beats death by Giro,' laughed Hardy. 'By the way, who's we?'

'At least I can answer that. So far you and me, but there's a short list in the glove compartment. Have a look.'

Hardy took out the list and scanned it.

'Moley Jackson. Fuck me, not that psycho.'

'He's a hard man and a good soldier.'

'He's a hard man, all right. Gives me the creeps. Ever find out how he got the nickname?'

'Moley? No, but I've often wondered.'

'Turns out that before he joined up he worked with a rough crew in south London. They were into nicking posh cars then selling them abroad.'

'And Moley did the mechanical work?'

'Mainly, until one day the gang tumble they've been stitched up by one of their own. They slapped the two main susses around but got nothing out of them. Moley drags the first bloke into his workshop and after ten minutes he's singing like a canary.'

'What did he do, for Chrissake?'

'Don't know, but all Moley went in with was the bloke and a pair of Mole grips.'

'Christ,' was all Carlisle could say. His mind was back in the seething heat of the Tehran cell. Suddenly he could feel the clammy hands of his torturers and smell the sweet stench of butter, cinnamon and garlic on their breath. He wanted to vomit.

He flicked the heater off and wound down the window.

'You OK, Pete?'

'Yeah, yeah, I'm all right.'

But Carlisle was wondering whether he would ever be all right, because the sickness he felt was partly self-revulsion. Secretly he was pleased by Hardy's story. Who could tell, they might just need Moley's gruesome talents on this trip. 'It's a dirty job but someone's got to do it,' he murmured to himself. But just how dirty? And how long before the dirt started to grow inside of him? That was the problem.

At about five they turned off the M1 and headed east.

'Where are we going?' asked Hardy.

'Norwich. Devaney and Gray hang their hats there.'

'Yeah, I saw their names on the list. What are they doing now?'

'Devaney, you call him Pug, don't you?'

'Yeah.'

'Well, he's boxing again and Gray's gone back to gambling.'

'What a pair,' said Hardy wistfully. His head was tilted back on his seat, and on his face was a look Carlisle knew well. It was the look that said a soldier was back in his past. Where the beer was served up in three-pint jars and gorgeous girls were cutting cards for the privilege of sitting on his face. Most importantly it was where his mates were. And all of them still alive. Hardy shook himself out of his daydream.

19

'I heard Pug got a bit wobbly after Longdon. Blamed himself for a load of stuff or something. That right?' he asked.

'Apparently, but then didn't we all?'

'Yeah, I reckon so.'

After that they said very little. There was not much to say.

They reached Pug Devaney's house by eight. Hardy stayed in the car as Carlisle walked up to the door. After two knocks the door was opened by a pretty blonde in her thirties. She looked square on at Carlisle and seemed to be reading his mind through sad, care-worn eyes.

'He's not here,' she said in a soft Scottish Lowlands accent.

For some reason Carlisle was taken aback by the woman and just stared stupidly at her. As he was about to speak she cut in.

'If you want him he's down at the Sports Village. Fighting, if that's what you call it.'

Before Carlisle had a chance to say a thing she closed the door without a word. He walked back to the car. Hardy's eyes were fixed on the house.

'Very nice, very nice indeed. Old Pug's done OK for himself by the look of it.'

'I'm not so sure about that,' Carlisle said darkly.

'Something up, Pete?'

'Might be,' replied Carlisle. And as he turned the car round he seemed to be staring into the beautiful sad eyes of Devaney's woman. Suddenly he realized they had been filled with hatred. 'Let's get down to this sports place and find out.'

Fifty pounds on the door was enough to get them both a seat close to the ringside. Pug's bout was underway as they sat down. What they saw appalled both men. Pug was backed into a corner by his opponent, who whipped brutal punches into his body and bloodstained head. All through the butchery he had a weird grin on his face as though he was enjoying the whole ritual. His best pal, Lenny Gray, was in his corner, screaming at his mate.

'Come on, Pug, do it, do it. You can murder him, Pug.'

Which was true. Anthony Devaney had been one of the finest physical specimens 3 Para had ever seen. Six foot two and built of something harder than mere muscle and bone, he was feared, admired and liked in equal measure by every man who ever knew him. No one doubted he was destined to be a champion. Until, that was, the grim events on Mount Longdon. What no one knew, except perhaps for Carlisle, who was beginning to get the picture, was that Pug was reliving those terrible hours of battle in the boxing ring in front of them. Every punch that smashed into his jaw was an Argentinian high-explosive shell ripping into their dugout. The roar of the crowd was the massive explosion that plumed men, guns and ammo into the freezing Falklands night.

It was 14 June 1982, the final night of the Longdon

assault. Pug had wriggled forty yards or so under heavy enemy defensive fire. He'd just flushed out a sniper who had them pinned down in a tricky area. As Pug turned to signal to the rest the first shell screamed over. It hit middle ground. Another came, then another. The fourth hit the dugout. Pug ran screaming back to his comrades only to find an executioner's pile of limbs and torsos. Precisely what Pug did after that no one could say. But whatever vengeance he wreaked it was never enough. He blamed himself for the deaths of his comrades and the punishment he was taking in the ring was only what he thought he was due.

Carlisle could stand no more. He walked to Pug's corner and said with calm authority, 'Gray, enough! Stop it.'

Gray sprang up from his seat and did precisely as Carlisle had ordered.

Back in the changing room Pug was slumped in a chair.

'You shouldn't have stopped it, sir. You shouldn't have stopped it. I could have taken more,' he groaned.

Carlisle knelt by the chair and stared into the man's glazed eyes.

'No, Pug, you're through with taking more, do you understand me? No more beatings, no more of that crap we just sat through. From now on you carry your guilt like the rest of us. If you're man enough.'

Carlisle stood up and walked to the other side of the room. Pug's head dropped to his chest and coin-sized drops of blood splashed his white trunks. The four ex-Paras stood in total silence as two whole minutes passed. Then Pug lifted his head.

'I'm man enough,' he said, a fire burning in his wild Irish eyes.

'Never doubted it, old son. Not for a minute. But to work. I've got a king's shilling on offer. Who's interested?'

'What's the SP?' asked Gray.

'Six of us against half an army.'

'We're in,' chimed Pug and Gray.

'The pay's five grand a week for as long as you stay alive to spend it.'

'Luncheon vouchers?'

'Naturally,' laughed Carlisle.

A massive grin spread over Pug's handsome features.

The men made contact arrangements, shook hands and parted.

As they sped down the M11 towards London, Hardy turned to Carlisle and said, 'That was a tight little speech back there, Pete. I'm impressed.'

'Put it down to genius.'

'Not that impressed,' said Hardy.

'You men, you're so fickle.'

Both men laughed.

Carlisle dropped Hardy at the safe house in Woodford Green known as the OK Hotel, then drove home. It was hotter back in London, and the sheets on the spare bed were soon clammy with Carlisle's sweat. He was dreaming that the six of them were in a clearing somewhere, and were being led by the hated Garvan. It turned out to be an ambush and one by one they were tied up and shot. Garvan was laughing loudly.

'Kill them slowly, they like it,' he was saying. Carlisle leapt at him and beat his head to a bloody pulp. He woke to find the bed in disarray and the teak bedside cabinet on its side. It was time to go. He phoned Hardy.

'Hardy, it's Peter Carlisle. We're on.'

'Give us a break, Pete, it's only three o'clock. I haven't finished me wank yet.'

'Be quicker next time.'

Two days later both men were aboard a scheduled flight to Athens. The plane was passing low over the Albanian Alps. Hardy looked down and smiled as he said, 'Fuck me, you were right. It *is* like the Westerns. Look, there are the vultures.'

Huge birds were wheeling in dizzy circles above the mountain tops.

'They're eagles, old son. We're in the Land of the Eagles.'

As Carlisle said this he looked down on the rocky terrain below with a terrible menace in his eye. Somewhere in those mountains was the man who had butchered his dearest friend. Carlisle was going to find him and make him wish he'd never been born.

4

Something unusual happened at Athens airport. A perfect landing; no bumps or thuds.

'Smooth or what?' said Hardy as he snapped his seat belt open.

'So far so good,' said Carlisle.

'That's what I like about you, Pete – the eternal optimist. A cheerful sod, that's what you are.'

'I'll be cheerful when the job's done and all your hairy arses are back in England. Until then let's play it straight. Incidentally, before your eyes pop out of your head . . .' Hardy's eyes were threatening to do just that, as he mentally undressed the delectable Swissair stewardess standing by the exit. 'If you remember, our cover is as two bumbling amateur ornithologists,' Carlisle added. 'We're on two weeks' holiday from our humdrum jobs and the only birds we're interested in are the ones that shit on your car just after you've finished waxing it. So look long and hard at Miss Switzerland down there. From now on we're shy, quiet boys. Got it?'

As the two men moved through the airport con-
course no one would have thought for a second
they were anything but what they were pretending
to be. Every detail had been attended to. Various parts of their clothing had been deliberately
distressed to mimic the wear caused by constant
use of bird-watching paraphernalia. They carried
specialist pocket telescopes, trade magazines and
fake diaries going back to the late seventies. Yet
for all the meticulous planning both men lifted the
ninety-pound suitcases with no effort, and moved
with the grace and ease of top-class athletes. Dead
giveaways for those with eyes to see.

As they ambled by, a dark-haired woman in her
thirties was struggling with a large suitcase. There
was a tearing noise as handle and suitcase parted.
She cursed in Greek. Hardy turned and knelt in an
instant. 'Don't worry, love,' he said with a grin as
he picked up the case. 'Christ! What's in here, Fort
Knox?'

The woman fussed over the case. 'Oh, please be
careful, you'll hurt yourself. It's too heavy.'

'It's done now,' said Hardy as he placed the dead
weight on to an empty trolley.

'Thank you so much,' the woman said. 'They are
presents from my mother.'

Hardy joined Carlisle and they walked towards the
exit. 'Presents from her mother! Fuck me, who's her
mother married to? King Kong? That bloody thing
weighed a ton.'

Back at the trolley the woman seemed to be composing herself until, that was, Carlisle and Hardy were out of sight. Then she paused and looked up and along the second-storey balcony. Her eyes met the steady gaze of a man draped casually over the railing. She made no more than the ghost of a nod. It said Carlisle and Hardy were the men they had been waiting for. Within seconds the man had melted into the crazy babble of the airport. When he reached the taxi rank he hailed a cab. The driver cut out of the waiting pack and, with perfect timing, glided up to the waiting Englishmen. He wound down his window and called to them, 'Taxi, gentlemen?'

'Now that's what I call timing,' Hardy laughed as he threw his case into the open boot. Carlisle followed him in silence. The taxi and its driver were straight out of a B-movie. The car was a high-winged monstrosity from the sixties, although the driver, with his thinning, slicked-back hair and pencil moustache, looked a much earlier vintage. Carlisle watched his every movement as he scurried round the car and checked the boot was shut.

'You OK, Pete? You look like there's something on your mind.'

'How'd he know we were English?'

'Huh?'

'He spoke to us in English. We could have been anything. Germans, Swedes, Dutch, anything.'

'What, dressed like this? Are you joking? Fuck

me, all we need is knotted hankies and we'd make a postcard.'

'Maybe,' was all Carlisle answered. His eyes were fixed on the driver. 'We want the Hotel Cotapaxi. Know where that is?'

The driver turned and with a puzzled look stuttered a broken sentence. 'I no . . . er, no speak English.'

Carlisle repeated the words loudly and clearly: 'Hotel Cotapaxi.'

After a pause a big grin spread over the driver's face.

'Cot-a-paxi, ah yes, Cotapaxi, yes, good.' Nodding and still grinning, he drove off.

Carlisle sat back and said conversationally, 'Hey spic-ball, me and my friend here, we fucked your sister and your mother last night. One in the mouth, one up the arse. They're a great fuck, the pair of them. Did you know that?' There was no response from the driver. He carried on whistling the Kim Wilde number that was on the radio as his impassive eyes skittered across the treacherous Athens highways. When Hardy tumbled what Carlisle was up to he turned to him.

'Well, Pete, he's either the best actor since Olivier or he's on the level and he really doesn't speak English.'

'Maybe.'

The Hotel Cotapaxi was from the same B-movie as the driver and his taxi. It was a white, three-storey building that shimmered in the searing afternoon sun. It had reached nearly 37° outside, but it felt like twice that inside. A roly-poly Greek stood sweating at the reception desk. He wore a surprisingly clean dark suit, and his fat hairy hands were weighed down with gold rings. He greeted them with their cover names. 'Ah! Mr Carpenter, Mr Henry! Welcome to the Hotel Cotapaxi.'

'Didn't the Eagles sing that one?' joked Hardy.

The fat man reached behind him and took a key from the board as Carlisle was signing the empty guest book.

'Slack period?' asked Carlisle.

'So so,' said the fat man, grinning.

As the rest of the formalities were finishing, the kitchen door, next to the desk, flew open and a rancid smell of fatty meat smacked both men in the face.

'Thank you, Mr Carpenter, Mr Henry. Will you be dining tonight?' the fat man asked ingratiatingly. The Englishmen looked at each other and declined the offer.

Once in their room they flopped down on spongy, metal-framed beds and Hardy mimicked the Greek.

'Un weel yoo bee daining toonaite?' He laughed aloud. 'You should have seen your face, Pete. What were they boiling up in that kitchen anyway? Dead cats?'

'Probably,' Carlisle replied vaguely. He looked worried.

Hardy himself was beginning to worry. He'd seen men, hard men, crack when you least expected it.

Maybe Carlisle was nearing that point. He decided to pour a drop of oil on troubled waters.

'Sorry about that business on the plane, Pete.'

'Eh?'

'The plane, that bird I was ogling. Guess I was way out of order. It's just, well, it all seems like play-acting so far.'

Carlisle turned on his side and paused. 'Is that right? Well, if it keeps you alive then just do it. Believe it or not this is one of the riskiest parts of the job.'

Hardy looked puzzled.

'You don't believe me, do you? OK, let me tell you about Jason Bannister. He was a good Marine, one of the best. Our cover was as middlemen in some shitty arms deal. The stuff was coming out of Russia. We were near to closing. I thought I was being dead clever when I sent him back to our hotel for some more coke. You know, sweeten the atmosphere and then in for the kill. I must have sounded a bit clipped or something – anyway Jason answered, "OK, sir." Remember, this is in front of apes who can barely speak English. Well, Bannister never came back from that little errand. When I found him he'd been garrotted. They'd carved "to sir with love" on his stomach. Judging by the amount of blood, he was alive when they did it. Ever since then I've been a firm believer in keeping up appearances, you might say.'

'Point taken,' said Hardy, as just the faintest of shadows passed over his face.

Around ten-thirty there was a knock on the door.

It was the fat man. Carlisle exchanged a few words with him and when he was gone turned to Hardy.

'Watch my back, Rich, there could be something up here.'

'What's the score?'

'Might be nothing. But we're the only guests in a flea-pit in the arsehole of Athens and all of a sudden the bloke we're supposed to be meeting is otherwise engaged.'

'What bloke?'

'We're meant to meet up with some bloke called Deamestru. He's supplying a vehicle and maybe hardware.'

'And?'

'According to our fat friend Mr Deamestru has gone fishing. He's sent his deputy. So cover me. He's coming up now.'

'Done.'

Deamestru's man was about thirty-five and of average height and build. All a bit too average, Carlisle was thinking as they shook hands.

'Mr Carpenter, how do you do. My name is Theakis and Mr Deamestru sends his sincere apologies but . . .'

'I'm sure he does, but as you'll appreciate, my companion and I are extremely tired. Could we just see the vehicle?'

'Ah yes, the vehicle, it is this way.' He pointed to a lay-by that was shadowy, strewn with debris and overlooked by two derelict warehouses. An ancient Mercedes van waited for him there.

'Could you drive it up here, please? I'd like to see how it runs,' said Carlisle.

'Sure,' Theakis replied, and walked straight over to the van.

Carlisle was impressed. It was obvious that here was a man who could think on his feet. It was time for Carlisle to do the same. There was definitely something going down here.

The van pulled up and Carlisle walked around, making the usual curious amateur observations. What he didn't comment on was the tip of a CZ automatic handgun that he saw peeking out from under a heavy canvas sheet in the back of the van. Almost certainly there was a hand attached to the gun. It was time for action.

'Looks fine. How much?'

'Well . . .'

Carlisle cut short the haggling and offered nearly double what he knew the vehicle was worth. Theakis agreed at once and Carlisle began to peel several $100 bills from a bulging money-belt. Then he hesitated.

'Could we, er . . . could we do this inside?'

'Sure.'

As they walked across the hotel lobby the fat man nodded at both men. He was wearing headphones that were plugged into a cheap-looking personal stereo. As they passed, Carlisle could hear the tinny sound of Abba's 'Dancing Queen'. His mind was in overdrive. Even so, he'd seen the first danger too late. Sandwiched between the two of them, if the fat man was in cahoots with Theakis then he was dead. But the fat man just drummed his fingers on the desk and whistled tunelessly to the music. He was clean.

In a millisecond Carlisle worked out what he would do in the place of his would-be assassin. It would be at the top of the stairs. A knockout blow, then a knife or silenced gun to the heart. They turned the bend on the stairs and Carlisle could feel his body becoming as hard and brittle as titanium. He knew the job must be done on the landing. Each stair was taking himself or Theakis closer to eternity.

At the third step along the landing Carlisle turned like a flash to find the butt of Theakis' gun about to crush his skull. He caught the man's wrist and snapped it like a carrot. His right arm closed round his neck and the Greek's legs lashed out in violent but pathetic lunges. The bedroom door flew open and Hardy yanked the bodies, locked as one, inside. In a last, desperate effort Theakis kicked out wildly and caught Hardy in the balls. Doubling in pain, Hardy drew his knife and thrust it into the man's belly and then up, under the ribcage, and straight into his heart. It was an expert job. No blood. No noise. Just the Greek's eyes half an inch from Hardy's – the whites still pure white, the pupils brown as tobacco, and both beginning to bulge from his head like tennis balls.

'Go like fuck, Rich. We've got about a minute,'

Carlisle rasped. 'There's a guy tooled up in the van. We've got to take him out, come on.'

Carlisle searched the body for more hardware. There was nothing. He threw the gun to Hardy.

'If he gets by me, then you've got one shot and that's it. These boys are pros.'

With miraculous calm Carlisle walked to the hotel entrance and then stopped and turned back as if he'd forgotten something. The second assassin burst through the door with the CZ levelled ready to kill. Carlisle had doubled back and was on the blind side of him as he entered. The side of Carlisle's hand powered into the man's throat. The blow smashed the third and fourth vertebrae, at the same time crushing the major blood vessels of the neck. In a few seconds the man was dead.

The sheer speed of events had shocked the fat man, whose mouth gaped like a hungry chick's. He stood and was yanking the headphones off when Hardy delivered a similar deadly blow to the back of his neck. He fell back in his chair with a long, wheezing sigh and then went quiet. His eyes had an astonished look like he'd just won a lot of money. The headphones lay on the ground and Abba played on but the fat man's fingers were still. They wouldn't be drumming to any more tunes. Hardy looked up, grinning.

'One shot, eh Pete?'

'He was friendly, Rich. You've just killed an inno-cent man.'

The two mercenaries stared dumbstruck at each

other. It seemed an eternity before Carlisle added, 'Come on, let's clean up and get out of here.'

The job done, they locked the hotel door and drove off in the van in search off a safe place to dump their grim cargo. Neither man said a word. They'd reached another shabby suburb when Carlisle suddenly wrenched the wheel round and they came to a halt. It was the edge of an industrial area and two massive skips stood by a factory under construction.

'This'll do,' Carlisle said in a cold, flat voice.

'What, all of them?'

'No, we'll take the fat man into the cathedral and hold a service. That suit you? Oh, and we'll pick some flowers on the way.'

'That's not funny, Pete.'

'Death rarely is, old son. But then I didn't kill him. Let's go.'

The two assassins were easy. But the fat man was at least eighteen stone and, strong as they were, they had to lever him over the rim of the skip. As they did a photograph fluttered from his jacket pocket. With a final push they rolled him in and covered the three bodies with some of the debris that was strewn all over the building site. Then Carlisle bent over and picked up the photograph. He held it up to the dim interior light as he drove the van out of the site. It was the fat man maybe twenty years ago. He was a lot thinner but still recognizable. Standing all around him were a tiny woman and an assortment of children that could only have been his. Hardy's eyes closed and his nostrils flared.

'You didn't fucking well tell me, Pete. You didn't say a word.'

'They'll sort out compensation. It's done quietly but dependants are always taken care of.'

'Does my conscience get compensation?'

'From now on you don't have a conscience, OK?'

Carlisle drove on through the sticky heat of the Athens summer night. He stopped by a public phone box and emptied a pile of change on to the shelf. The call soon grew heated and Hardy could hear his pal making some pretty nasty threats to whoever was at the other end.

'Friend of yours?' he asked.

'That piece of shit Garvan.'

'I don't believe it! What's that cunt doing out here?'

'He's not out here. His type never are. That was his special line. He got all narked we'd woken him. Anyway he's given me another contact for hardware. Let's get over there.'

Hardy didn't like what he was hearing. 'You mean that arsehole sets up our contacts?'

'Yep. And the funny thing is . . .' Carlisle slipped the van into third and a grinding like the death throes of a Victorian mangle accompanied his action. 'Shit, this old beast's more clapped than I thought. Hope she gets us through the mountains.'

Hardy dropped the question about Garvan. What he had just heard alarmed him even more.

'What fucking mountains? The plan was to rendez-vous with the rest of the lads in Salonika. There's no bastard mountains there.'

'Calm down, Rich, there's been a change of plan.'

Hardy snapped. He wrenched the wheel of the van over and as it was pulling up he stuck the muzzle of his CZ into Carlisle's throat.

'What change of plan?'

Carlisle turned and faced Hardy with a rare calm only certain men can muster. Hardy's granite features showed a dangerous mixture of anger and panic.

'OK, Rich, spit it out,' Carlisle said quietly.

A dam burst in Hardy's brain and he ranted and screamed at Carlisle as he pushed the handgun ever harder against his throat. Carlisle knew what it was all about. Hardy was a lethal killing machine. But he was a decent man, an honest soldier. He hadn't been prepared for the slip-up back at the hotel.

'That fat bloke, Rich, I didn't know he was friendly until we took out the first bastard upstairs. OK, it was my mistake.'

'Your mistake. Your fucking mistake! So some poor bastard's gotta die 'cos you make a mistake, and his only crime in life was overeating. You sloppy fucker, I ought to blow your brains out.'

Carlisle turned away and stared down the litter-strewn road ahead. Rats were gnawing on the remains of take-away meals tossed idly from passing cars. What a place to die, he thought to himself. But he had to face Hardy down.

'Afraid you got it wrong, Rich. His only crime was being in the wrong place at the wrong time. Now you'd better use that gun 'cos he's not coming back, and well . . . yeah, that was my mistake. You never make mistakes?'

Hardy's grip tightened on the automatic, but his shoulders began to tremble and his head dropped slightly as he began to sob quietly.

'Poor fucker. He had kids. Lovely little kids.'

Carlisle didn't answer – there was no point. He eased the van smoothly into the flow of traffic.

'Get some shut-eye. It'll take us about an hour to get to this place.'

'What then?'

'Then we tool up and get the fuck out of here.'

They threaded their way through a maze of streets even seedier than before and eventually pulled up by a hotel that made the Cotapaxi look like the Ritz. A sign half hanging off the wall claimed ludicrously that 'luxury accommodation' was on offer. Two girls painted up like clowns and wearing thigh-length shiny boots but little else stood smoking beneath a red neon sign in Greek.

Hardy was still rubbing his eyes from a deep sleep. Then the place came into focus.

'Looks like a whorehouse.'

'Yeah. But then we're not going to get Kalashnikovs from a convent, are we?'

Carlisle jumped from the van and was joined by Hardy.

'Got the handgun?'

'Check.'

'OK, we'll leave the wagon open in case we have to leg it. Stick close. This one'll be gloves off. By morning those bodies will start getting high and we'll be hotter by the minute.'

The two men strode by the girls and into the front office.

A sleazy character welcomed them with a cringing false smile.

'You speak English?' asked Carlisle.

The man shrugged his shoulders with another forced smile. Carlisle ignored him and went on, 'We English, we need bang-bang.' With two fingers he crudely mimicked a gun. The man beamed at them.

'Ah, you flick-flick,' and he motioned even more crudely with his own fingers, rubbing them quickly together.

'No,' said Carlisle, grabbing the man's lapel with one hand and pulling a gun from the inside of his jacket with the other. He held the gun to the man's head. 'No, we mean bang-bang.' He lowered the barrel to the man's gaping mouth. 'Now, let's try it one more time. Do you speak English?'

The man nodded. A huge friendly grin spread over Carlisle's face. 'Of course you do. OK, now let's go.' They bundled him into the front of the van and roared away. The two girls waved their cigarettes at the van in a friendly goodbye.

'Wave back, you cunt,' said Hardy with a prod in

the ribs with his CZ. The man did as he was told.
'Good boy.'

They pulled up by a warehouse complex some ten
miles away. The man was shaking so much it took him
several minutes to get the locks open but eventually
the door swung wide and, beyond another door inside,
they found enough ordnance to win World War III.

'My, my, Grandma, what big anti-tank guns you've
got.' Hardy grabbed a shell and looked over at
Carlisle. 'We taking any of this stuff?'

'Just carry-weapons, Rich. Two of those Kalashnikovs, the Browning automatics and all the ammo we
can manage.'

Hardy toyed with a high-explosive grenade. With
the look of a naughty boy he implored Carlisle, 'Come
on, Pete, just a couple. You know they help me sleep
better at night.'

'OK, purely for medicinal purposes then.'

They loaded up and roared off northwards out of
the sweltering city.

5

They soon left behind them the grey industrial towers of the outskirts of Athens. As the beautiful Greek countryside opened out, the atmosphere between them began to improve, becoming light and joky, like the old days.

Hardy turned to their reluctant passenger and said, 'Everything all right then, mate?'

The man shrugged his shoulders in a bemused way as if to say he didn't understand. The ploy infuriated Carlisle. Hadn't this arsehole realized that if they'd wanted to waste him they'd have done it back in the warehouse, or did he think they wanted the company of a pimp on their long journey northwards? Even more irritating to Carlisle was the fact that the pimp was underestimating him. Christ! Did he think Carlisle had forgotten that his attempt to play dumb had been rumbled only an hour earlier? Carlisle decided that it was time for a bit of fun. He looked over to Hardy, jerked his head towards the Greek and winked mischievously.

'So what are we going to do with this one then – waste him or what?'

The effect was immediate. The pimp twitched in his seat and clenched his hands the way back-seat drivers do on tricky bends.

Hardy stretched over the man's shoulder and whispered to his mate with mock seriousness.

'Steady on, Pete, he speaks the lingo you know.'

'No, we're OK on that score. He's dumb, didn't you notice?'

'Oh well, in that case . . .' Hardy's face beamed as he went on. 'The thing is, Pete, we could kill him if you want but well . . . I'm so randy at the moment I'd fuck a pig with a bonnet on. Don't get me wrong, he's not my type really, but what the hell, he's a man, so howsabout a bit of fun first?'

The pimp winced at this and when Carlisle nudged him he nearly jumped out of his seat. The smell of the man nearly made Carlisle throw up. But he still managed to say, as though he meant it, 'Nice eyes. Don't you think so, Rich?'

'They'll do. Come on, Pete, pull over.'

Carlisle drove down the nearest dusty track and pulled up by a secluded grove. He killed the engine and the pimp turned to him like a dog that had already been beaten. 'You want sex?' he whimpered. 'I get you nice girls. Nice dirty girls, they . . .'

Hardy whirled him round on his seat as he spoke. 'Girls! You pervert, get out of here.'

He hauled him out of the van in one movement

42

and kicked his backside so hard he lifted him off the ground. 'I'll give you girls. Now get those trousers off – and the frilly knickers. Now!'

The pimp did as he was told, pleading in Greek all the time. Carlisle could no longer contain himself, and erupted into laughter. As he rolled the window down the man was still babbling.

'I think he's saying to be gentle with him, Rich.'

Hardy threw the pimp's shoes at him. 'Get those on. Your feet stink and I'm not about to fuck a man with stinking feet, got it?'

The pimp did as he was told. As he hopped about on one foot the van turned round and Hardy jumped aboard, taking the pimp's clothes with him. Carlisle leant from the window, pulling $100 bills from his money-belt.

'OK, you come here. That's what we owe you for the hardware.' He dropped the bundle of notes on the floor. 'If you get a phone call from a piece of shit even smellier than yourself his name'll be Garvan. You can tell him that we paid you in full now, can't you?'

'Oh yes, in full. I will tell him yes, you were honest men, good men. Yes, but please, let me have just my trousers. Please?'

Carlisle made no reply but opened another compartment of the money-belt. He took out a dollar bill and handed it to the pimp.

'That's for you. Get a life. There should be some change. Keep it.'

As they pulled off both men noticed two boys of

twelve or thirteen standing at the side of the road and
laughing at the bony figure wearing nothing but his
crocodile-skin shoes. The van clattered into third gear
and Carlisle glanced in the rear mirror. In it he saw
that a fat mama had got hold of the pimp. She looked
twice as wide as she was tall and had arms as thick
as her legs. With one meaty forearm she pinned the
man to the ground and with the other started beating
him about the head with one of his own shoes. If it
was possible Carlisle began to laugh even louder than
Hardy.

They joined the heavy flow of traffic heading north.
To their right was the sun, oozing blood-red from the
earth. The fragrant smell of a million flowers drove all
odours from the van. It seemed almost like a holiday.
They turned off for petrol. As Hardy fed the tank his
mate strolled across to pay. Just then an ancient truck
pulled away and back-fired. Both men flinched and
Hardy threw himself against the side of the van. The
holiday was over.

'So why are we shortcutting Salonika?'

'Because your old Uncle Pete smells a bit of a rat,
that's why.'

'What sort?'

'The smelly type,' Carlisle laughed.

'No, come on, Pete, level with me. So far I've been
like a spare prick at a wedding.'

Carlisle went on chuckling, but then his eyes glanced
down at the dashboard. There was the photo of the
fat man from the Cotapaxi. Surrounded by his wife

and chubby children, his image filled Carlisle with a terrible gloom.

'Yeah, I'm sorry, you're right.' Carlisle paused and took a deep breath. 'OK then, I'll tell you everything I know. Let's get it right from the beginning though. Everything so far has been kosher, OK?'

'Check.'

'I'll go through it. Our six-man team is tasked with a search-and-destroy mission. As I said on the plane, our cover will be as a party of British bird-watchers.'

'What, all of us? Including Pug Devaney?'

'Like I said, all of us. But don't interrupt for a minute. The plan is we amble round looking and acting pretty dim but all the while gathering intelligence on the two major Albanian families. And for family read private army. When the time's right we'll be given coordinates on three arms dumps hidden deep in the Albanian mountains. We tool up and blow the fuckers into outer space. And that's about it. Any questions?'

'Only the obvious one. Who planted the arms dump in Albania and why aren't they finishing the job themselves? Surely if you can get the sort of ordnance we're going to need into a place like Albania, then you must have the nous to finish the job.'

'Rich, I've underestimated you. With your brains you should have at least made lance-corporal.'

'Cheeky bastard.'

'OK, bullshit aside, you've hit it in one. There's something funny about this job. It revolves around this contact in Salonika.'

Just as he said this a sign for that city flashed by them, in Greek above and English below.

'Seventy kilometres, that's only about forty miles in old money. Why don't we drop by and have a little drink with the lads?' suggested Hardy.

'That's just what we can't do, Rich. Once we hit Salonika we'll be under orders from some bloke called Tomarzo. I've never even heard of him, and I don't like that.'

'Who would? But he must be kosher. Hasn't he got some flash security clearance? They don't give them away in Christmas crackers.'

'Maybe,' came Carlisle's stock reply. 'But I don't think I'll give Mr Tomarzo the benefit of the doubt. Anyway I'm pretty sure he doesn't know where the fuck we are, so let's take a little peek at Albania for ourselves.'

With that he swung on to the right-hand slip road and took a huge left-hand loop which headed towards the border and away from Salonika.

It took two hours to reach the border and by the time they got there both men were feeling bushed. By the ramshackle building stood a collection of ill-dressed border guards.

Carlisle drew up to the single inspection bay and stuck his head out of the window.

'Good afternoon,' he said in his most inoffensive manner. The look he got back from the guard told him this one really didn't speak a word of English.

Carlisle took two $100 bills and put one in each of the passports. This was a language the guard did understand. He looked the van up and down cursorily and waved them on.

'So that's how it's done,' said Hardy.

'Just improvise – that's the name of the game, Rich,' Carlisle replied, then added, as he moved the vehicle forward, 'Hang about. This looks trickier.'

A group of stern-looking young guards approached them as they pulled up at the Albanian checkpoint. They all wore smart grey uniforms that must have been in mothballs since Stalin died.

'Passports,' snapped the one in front.

Carlisle handed over both passports and waited for an answer. He got one.

'Get out,' said the guard.

Both men did as they were told and tried their best to look bemused. Their credentials were soon established as the van was ransacked and the ground littered with binoculars, bird-identification books and maps. But then an uneasy silence followed and Hardy whispered to Carlisle as the guards walked round the vehicle.

'The Browning's taped to the underside of the middle seat. I could waste the lot of them, Pete.'

'And go where? No, leave it to me.'

'Excuse me, officer, is there a problem?' Carlisle asked politely.

The guard stared at him for several seconds, then asked, 'How long will you stay in Albania?'

'No more than two weeks. We . . .'

The guard looked into the rear of the van and when he found the door locked turned to Carlisle.

'You have a lot of equipment for two weeks. May I see it, please?'

'By all means.' Carlisle seemed to fumble for a key when a $10 bill fluttered to the ground. He picked it up and looked quizzically at the guard. 'Must be yours,' he said in an almost servile manner.

'Perhaps,' answered the guard as he turned to the rest of his men, who had congregated by the office door. He turned back to Carlisle with a questioning look on his face. Carlisle played dumb and then said with mock surprise, 'Oh, oh, I see, er, how many?'

'There are eight more.'

'So that will be . . . let me see . . . if I give you a $100 bill do you have change by any chance?'

The guard snatched the hundred and returned with the $10 bill a wad of Albanian notes thick enough to choke a donkey. 'Enjoy your holiday,' he said and waved them through.

'Now that's what I call Marxism in action,' said Hardy. 'See the way they got a little taste of the loot? Nearly moved me to tears.'

'And he'd have been moved to tears if they hadn't got their share. These poor sods are desperate.'

'And cheap.'

'Don't be fooled. Know what the annual salary runs at out here? I'll tell you: about $200. Those boys are rolling in it by Albanian standards.'

'So $100 apiece and we could have sailed through no problem.'

'No, $100 apiece and we'd have signed our death-warrants. Not many people would kill for a small fortune. But many would kill for a large one. And to your average Albanian that's precisely what we've got.'

'Pete, you think of everything.'

'I like to think so.'

It was early evening by the time the van was melting into the darkening brown of the foothills of the Albanian Alps. In the rear-view mirror the harsh lights of the border post twinkled briefly and vanished.

Electricity was beginning to tingle through Carlisle's body, and as the dark wrapped round them he could almost smell his prey.

6

Under a dim lamp the two men prised open their field rations and ate as though there was no tomorrow.

'Amazing how hungry you get,' said Hardy. 'But I can't believe I'm eating this crap again.'

Carlisle said nothing. Almost in rhythm with the chirruping of the night insects his powerful jaws scythed through the tough dried meat. Hardy tried once again to draw him into conversation.

'The thing is, the army's got better guns, better explosives, better intelligence – you name it. Yet the compo rations still taste like they've come out of a bloody mummy's tomb.'

Carlisle smiled, gulped down the requisite amount of water and turned over in his sleeping-bag. He checked the safety-catch on his 9mm auto and made himself comfortable. 'Lights out, Rich,' was all he said.

'Sweet dreams.'

Within a minute Hardy was in the midst of his. But for Carlisle sleep didn't come so easily. His mind had jammed on Hardy's predictable comments about the compo rations. The words 'better intelligence' kept bumping about in his mind. Just who were 'Intelligence'? And who among them had tapped the highest security clearance into the British government's computer for Nicomedes Tomarzo? A man he'd never even heard of. It didn't make sense. He knew men in every combat unit across the globe, having fought alongside most of the bastards. But he didn't recall any of them ever mentioning the name Tomarzo. Yet someone had given the man a 2/AA clearance. It was driving Carlisle crazy. Who could it have been? A name was beginning to harden in his mind. But for now he'd let it stay there. His right arm was outside the sleeping-bag. As he slipped into dreams his grip tightened on the 9mm auto.

'Wakey, wakey, sleeping beauty,' said Carlisle, handing Hardy a steaming cup of tea. The clear morning sun was burning his eyes. He rubbed them as he sat up. 'Magic,' Hardy croaked as he reached out to take the first sacred brew of the morning. 'Just carry on as usual, Rich. We'e being watched,' Carlisle said casually.

Instinctively Hardy's eyes darted left and right over Carlisle's shoulder.

'Where?'

'Never mind where. Just act normal. Do something, laugh.'

Hardy broke into a jolly laugh. 'Ha, ha, so tell me, where are the fuckers? Ha, ha.'

Keeping up the same act, Carlisle explained that at

least two 'bodies' were covering them from a vantage-point thirty yards south-west. Hardy clocked them as he took in the rest of the plan. Carlisle counted. 'One . . . two . . . three . . .' He spun round on his right leg, letting his body fly in the same direction. While in mid-air he pumped the whole magazine at the vantage-point. At least five rounds split and shattered rock over the concealed bodies. It gave Hardy the vital two seconds he needed. He pounced from his sleeping-bag, grabbed his Browning and emptied the mag at the same spot. Both men regrouped on the blind side of the van. Hardy slid the two Kalashnikovs from the safe unit and they trained them on the same target. There followed an eerie silence of around twenty seconds.

'Have we got them?' asked Hardy.

'Don't think so. We'd have heard something by now. Unless we landed bull's-eyes, and that's not likely.'

A further silence followed and experience told both men that it was all clear. Nevertheless they were still cautious as they approached, but as they had guessed, the bird had flown. Behind the rock cover a gully dropped away to a thick pine wood.

'Tail them?' asked Hardy.

'Not worth it. Let's get out of here.' As they packed, Carlisle turned to his oppo and said, 'No wisecracks, Rich. That was good work. I'm impressed.'

'Thanks. You weren't bad yourself.'

*   *   *

52

The heat rose with fearsome intensity as the van groaned and rumbled along the mountain route that skirted the eastern edge of the country. The rough track that passed for a road was deeply rutted and potholed from heavy use, and the two men's sweating bodies were thrown all over the cab.

'Mountain goats didn't make this lot,' grumbled Hardy.

'Dead right, but at least it confirms intelligence and we're not on a wild-goose chase. Someone must be carrying some pretty tasty cargo to make them take this route. Could only be grade-A heroin.'

Hardy whistled. His body tensed. He too now felt that the hunt was on.

The condition of the roads and the age of the van made progress slow. What people they saw were mostly barefoot and poverty-stricken, while on higher ground they often caught sight of sheep that seemed to slither over the rocks effortlessly.

'Wouldn't mind roasting one of them tonight,' said Hardy.

'And have every mountain peasant join us for supper? Stick to your compo rations, Ri . . .'

Carlisle braked violently, leapt out of the van and ran back a few yards. He returned with a large broken wing-nut. 'Recognize that?'

Hardy whistled even louder than before.

'Fuck me, that's off a Scorpion HAV. It springs the sudden-release unit.'

'I told you, Rich, you could have made lance-corporal. You're spot on.'

Carlisle looked back along the shimmering road and said, 'This is the second part of the jigsaw. We know now that there's heavy armoured vehicles on the loose here. I'll bet my fee for this job there's a lot else besides them. Let's go.'

Hardy was beginning to understand the pattern of mercenary life. Action one minute and then tedium. After their discovery the pair spent the rest of the day and half of the next in routine and fruitless surveillance. Then, at around two-thirty that afternoon, everything changed.

Hardy was at the wheel as the van toiled up yet another steep stretch of the tortuous mountain road.

'Pull off, Rich,' Carlisle shouted.

Hardy's response was immediate. They forked left from the main road, which cut steeply to the east. The track had looked safe at first glance but to the left was a perilous thousand-foot drop. Hardy nursed the van along the treacherous track until they reached a tumbledown shepherd's hut. The engine stopped and Carlisle announced, 'Yep, perfect.'

'For what?'

'To get two monkeys off our backs. That pair from two days ago – was it Friday? Anyway, they've been trailing us for the last fifteen miles. They're amateurs but we can't risk it.'

'Who are they?'

'Must be border guards. My guess is the Albanian

ones. The Greeks would have fucked off home by now.'

As he spoke Carlisle raised his high-powered binoculars to his eyes. In his vision was a single grey-uniformed figure. Imprinted on his brain was a new enemy.

'Can't we just warn them?'

'If a full mag from a CZ, followed by the same from a Browning, isn't a warning, then you tell me what is. Afraid we've got a job to do here, Rich.'

'Look, Pete, if they're amateurs like you say, I vote we just scare them and move on. They're just desperate for money, that's all. They probably don't mean to harm us . . .'

Hardy didn't finish. A high-velocity round singed his forehead and ripped a hole the size of a football in the roof of the stone hut. In doing so it threw down a great clod of ancient dirt, which hit Hardy full in the face. Both men hit the ground and as Hardy looked up Carlisle burst out laughing at the sight of him. Even though the danger was acute he couldn't stop himself. Grinning broadly he said, 'You've got a point, Rich. Let's get down there and have a little chat with those boys. I don't think they mean us any harm either.'

'Ha, ha. But I'll tell you what, they're not bad shots for amateurs, are they, you clever bastard.'

'They just got lucky, that's all, and their luck's about to run out.'

Carlisle was on the blind side of the border guards at the rear of the van. He pulled out a loaded Kalashnikov AK47 and threw it to Hardy.

'Give me a couple of covering shots, Rich. I'm making a run for the hut.'

Once in the hut Carlisle set to work. From a bag he'd loaded from the van he uncoiled some strong nylon fishing line, which he ran to the back of the hut. Then he found a V-shaped branch behind the hut and jammed a grenade in the cleft. He waited. After an hour or so Hardy called out to him, 'What's up?'

'Nothing,' answered Carlisle. 'So far so good. Any movement down there?'

'No.'

'OK then, get over here – fast.'

As Hardy made his run two high-velocity rounds zipped past him.

'Patient bastards, aren't they? I thought they might have gone home,' he hissed.

'Don't worry, their patience will run out and then we'll nail the fuckers. Just keep the road covered. Don't let them get the high ground.'

As soon as night fell Carlisle wriggled to the front of the hut and laid a trip-wire. He fed it to the back of the building with the fishing line. Then he whispered to Hardy, who still had the road square in his night sight, 'Rich, fall back. We're going to have a quarrel, you and me.'

'A what? Have you lost your marbles?'

'Listen, we're going to have a barney and you're going to shoot me. OK?'

'You been drinking in there or what?'

'Cut the crap, Rich, and just do as I say.'

Hardy backed into the hut with his eye still glued to the night sight. Carlisle gave him the plan. The two of them set about punching a hole in the back of the hut just big enough to wriggle through.

Down the road, less than a hundred yards from the hut, three Albanian border guards – not two as the mercenaries had thought – were about to begin their assault. They'd argued all afternoon and into the early evening but were now convinced that the two Englishmen were holed up and desperate. They'd seen Carlisle dive in with a bag. Since no further shots had been fired they took this to be food. They were about to close in and riddle the hut with bullets when they heard a violent argument flare up. In the cooling night air the sound of a fist smashing into flesh was unmiskable. Then two shots rang out, followed by a scream. There was a third shot, some low moaning and then silence.

The three guards conferred rapidly. It was clear that the Englishmen had killed each other. Two of the men were already planning what they would spend their share of the money on. The third wanted to wait but the others would hear none of it. They ran along the path to the hut, looked uneasily at its black mouth and then sprayed it with bullets. They agreed as they walked over Carlisle's trip-wire to cut the third man out, and if necessary kill him if he caused trouble. After all, wasn't it they who'd taken the initiative? He'd have waited all week.

They shuffled about in the darkness looking for the

two corpses. Hardy and Carlisle were at the rear of the hut and safe on high ground. The two guards were busy confirming to each other that 'Fortune favours the brave' when Carlisle jerked the fishing line and the HE grenade did its work.

The flash from the blast showed a ghastly shower of human remains. Hardy slapped Carlisle on the back.

'Fucking brill, mate, fucking brill. Master plan complete.'

'Not bad, though I say it myself,' said Carlisle, grinning. The two men scrambled down to the hut and were still on a high as they checked the van for damage. Then, from nowhere, a brilliant tracer flare turned the night sky into daylight.

'What the fuck!' they said almost as one. After feeling briefly like gods, they were suddenly helpless, toyed with by some unseen lethal hand.

Both men sprang into the defence mode, fully aware each second was vital. The flare hung above them for around fifteen seconds, and in that time they pushed the van under the cover of the remains of the hut and hid themselves in gullies on the high ground. The angry, fizzing noise of an HE shell preceded a fierce burst near them, the physical shock it delivered leaving both men unconscious. Like mice they had been swiped by the cat's paw.

7

When Carlisle came to he felt like he'd done fifteen rounds with Mike Tyson. Shapes, sounds and smells flooded his brain but in not quite the right order. He sat up and immediately vomited.

'Ah, breakfast,' groaned Hardy, who had come round moments earlier.

'Christ, what hit us?'

'Three HE shells, and strictly for the record, Pete, they missed. The van's taken a scratch, though.'

This bit of news roused Carlisle.

'Fuck it. What's the damage?'

'Shrapnel. It's taken out one of the rear wheels, and the radiator'll need a bit of patching but that's the main stuff.'

'Thank God for that.'

'Oh, and there's me – you remember little old me, don't you? Well, I've had a touch of the old severe body trauma and maybe some broken bones but . . .'

'Sorry, Rich,' Carlisle cut in. 'That was pretty stupid of me. Bloody stupid.'

'Just pulling your plonker, mate. I'll live. I'll get a brew on. How's yourself?'

'Better than dead,' answered Carlisle.

He stretched, then watched Hardy pottering about. The strength and resilience of the British fighting man never ceased to amaze him. Here was a man whose body must feel like it's been through a cement-mixer. Yet Carlisle knew that if the order was to force-march fifty miles that same day then Hardy would do it to the inch. For all the banter, he felt privileged just to know the man.

'Rich,' he called over to him.

'What?'

'I'll make the tea.'

It took them most of the day to get the van fit to pass muster. Even so, it was still touch and go.

'The rad's shot, Pete. It'll hold for a while but that's it. Where are we anyway?'

Carlisle took the map from the glove compartment and spread it out on the bonnet in the glaring afternoon sun.

'Let's see now. We're about here.' His finger pointed to a road deep in the mountains west of Lake Ohrid, which divided part of Albania from Kosovo. He was deep in concentration. 'How many miles is the rad good for?' he asked Hardy, who replied, 'Should get us back to the border. Don't know about Salonika, though.'

'We're not going to the border. Those shells came,

by my estimation, from about twelve miles north-west. I want to see who threw them at us.'

Hardy knew in a moment two things for certain. First that Carlisle's intended course of action was extremely dangerous. Secondly that nothing on earth would change his mind. He'd seen that same look during the final assault on Longdon. After thirty-two hours of continuous combat duty the platoon had been pinned down by Argentinian sniper fire. They only had to keep cover and wait for artillery to soften the target. Carlisle turned to his platoon and said, 'We've got a choice, lads. We can dig in and let some crapheads take the credit or go for the bastards.'

Carlisle, Devaney, Gray and Hardy, by some mira-cle, took the sniper position. Devaney got an HV wound and a commendation. The rest of them cher-ished the memory of seeing one of 3 Para's finest fighting men enter into legend.

'I can't guarantee the wheels, Pete,' said Hardy, snapping out of his daydream.

'Then we'll walk if need be. Come on, I've got a feeling there's someone up there I want to meet.'

'Friend of yours?'

'Not exactly.'

The someone Carlisle was thinking of was the man called Khodja. Carlisle knew that he had to find him quickly. The hatred that was building up inside him would burst out soon. And that might just occur at a time lethal to himself and the men he commanded.

As they cleared the last of the kit Hardy spotted a

body lying about fifteen yards from the hut, towards the road. He walked cautiously to where it lay.

'Hey, Pete, seen this?'

Both men looked down at the corpse, dressed in an Albanian border guard's uniform. A single black hole in his forehead showed how the man had died.

'Shrapnel,' said Carlisle.

'So we got two of them and then one of those HE shells must have plugged this cunt.'

Carlisle smiled. He knew what Hardy was thinking, that their brilliant plan hadn't been so brilliant after all. Had the shells not been targeted on the hut then the dead man in front of them would very likely have killed them both in their sleep.

'About time we had a touch of luck,' Carlisle concluded. 'Let's get in the van and get out of here.'

The point Carlisle had referred to might have been twelve miles in a straight line but as the mountain road steepened it twisted and turned more all the time. They'd covered thirty-three miles when Carlisle pulled over and took cover in a pine wood.

'What do you reckon, Rich?'

'Fucked if I know. We've scoured every track and gulley between the hut and here and there's no sign of a fucking thing. Just more mountains and sodding goat shit.'

'It's got to be here. It's got to.'

'What, for Christ's sake? We don't even know what we're looking for.'

'We'll know when we find it,' Carlisle grinned

wickedly. 'Come on, you lazy bastard, let's get this van camouflaged. We're going walkies.'

It took them half an hour to hide the van, but they did it so well that Hardy never believed they'd find it again.

'If it's got your old socks in, it shouldn't be too hard to sniff out,' Carlisle teased him. 'Now let's tool up. We'll take the handguns and a full mag each. Leave the Kalashnikovs here. We'll travel light – sleeping-bags, bit of compo and that's it. Oh, and give me your binocular case.'

Hardy handed it over, and Carlisle gently placed two grenades inside. 'Just in case,' he said.

With only about two hours of light left they had still found only abandoned shepherds' huts, more pine woods and here and there small shrines. There was no sign of anything that resembled a military installation.

'I think we imagined those shells last night, Pete.'

'Know what, I almost believe you. Shit!'

'I ought to say, mate, apart from that rad being on the way out, we haven't got much compo left either.'

Carlisle ignored the warning. His eyes were moving restlessly over the rough mountain terrain.

'The bastards are near, I know it. I can almost smell them. I get a feeling, Rich, and it's never wrong.'

'Look, Pete, I know you're in charge, but fuck it, we could die waiting in these mountains.'

Suddenly the realization of defeat spread gloomily over Carlisle's face.

'You're right, Rich. Fuck it, you're right. But . . . look, let's bed down here and take a different route back in the morning. That'll be our last throw of the dice. OK?'

'Never say die,' said Hardy, grinning broadly.

It was always the same in remote places. There seemed to be more stars than you ever imagined. Hardy lay wrapped in his sleeping-bag and counted twenty-three before he fell fast asleep.

He woke to find a large, powerful hand smothering his mouth. It was Carlisle's. Carlisle had a finger to his own mouth, urging silence. When he was sure Hardy knew the score he gently took his hand away and motioned with his thumb.

They had slept in a wide gully, and over the top of it, to the east, they could hear a great commotion. In the background they could make out the rumbling of a tank engine. Both men peered gingerly over the rim of the gully and could not believe what they saw.

'Christ Al-fucking-mighty, what the hell is that?' whispered Hardy. Neither had dreamt of anything like it before.

Down at the end of the ground sloping from the gully was a concrete fortress that jutted from the mountainside and was about fifty yards wide and thirty deep. It seemed to be two storeys high – there were no windows – except where a large dome flanked by two smaller ones rose another twenty feet from the flat roof. The only visible entrance was a heavy armour-plated door the like of which Carlisle had seen only on nuclear fallout shelters.

On the open ground in front of the fortress was a group of soldiers. They were shouting at two bound prisoners who had been led out from inside, and then they started to beat them savagely. The prisoners screamed out over and over again two words which sounded to the Englishmen like '*nadimeh*' and '*mersherreh*'. Their cries were ignored. One of the soldiers beat a prisoner's thigh with a thick baton. The sickening crack and the man's screams left them in no doubt that his leg was broken. The other soldiers cheered and laughed. They turned the prisoner over and held him so that the second leg could be smashed. On the second blow the poor creature soiled his trousers, which gave rise to even more laughter. The soldiers pointed to the pool of shit and taunted the man. They rubbed his face in it and then kicked his broken legs. The screams were terrible. He repeated a different word: '*Shcarda, shcarda.*' Carlisle began to shake. He ducked back into the gully.

'The fucking bastards.'

'Careful, Pete, for Christ's sake. They're only twenty yards away. You'll blow the whistle.'

Carlisle wasn't listening. He rocked to and fro and began to mutter. What Hardy didn't know was that his oppo had been thrown back into the grim past. As they smashed the other prisoner's legs each blow and each scream gave more life to Carlisle's own obscene memories. The faces of his Iranian torturers began to dance in front of his eyes.

'He's pleading to die, Rich,' he hissed through trembling lips. 'The poor bastard, pleading . . .'

'Pete, for God's sake, they're going to hear and we'll be taking their place.'

Then came a scream more terrible than anything they had ever heard. Hardy almost leapt in the air. When he looked over he saw that the first prisoner's genitals had been cut away and the most brutal-looking of the soldiers was stuffing them into his mouth. Then they started to take pot-shots at him for what seemed to be idle fun.

Hardy had seen enough, and was about to vomit. He turned from the scene to be met by Carlisle's face an inch from his own. The look on Carlisle's face said it all. Even though he was still trembling there seemed to be a perfect stillness about him. He stared into Hardy's eyes for a full minute. No words were needed.

'I'm with you, Pete,' said Hardy quietly. He pulled out his CZ, kissed the barrel and waited for the word. Carlisle clipped the magazine into his Browning, then took one of the grenades from the case and pulled the pin.

'Go!' he yelled.

The force of his voice made the soldiers turn as one so that they looked for a moment like a row of skittles. The grenade took care of the gang by the armoured door. About a dozen of them were blown high into the air. Before the last body had landed both men had nearly covered the twenty yards between them and the remaining torturers. Both guns opened up on full auto. Some thirty Albanian corpses were scattered over the ground in under three seconds. Carlisle rushed to the castrated prisoner. The man was only semi-conscious and as his blood-drenched head shook from side to side his penis dropped from his mouth and on to his chest.

He looked up at Carlisle and croaked, 'Shcarda, shcarda.'

Carlisle had never seen a more pitiful sight. He held the man's hand and raised the reloaded Browning to his forehead. A single bullet sent him to merciful oblivion.

Seconds later a strident alarm screeched out from the fortress. Carlisle ignored it and instead turned to look for the castrator. Dead faces look so alike that it took him valuable moments to find his prey. Then more time to mash the soldier's head to a greasy, unrecognizable stain on the ground.

Hardy dragged him away but only just in time as the massive door was sliding open and the first armoured vehicle rumbled out to destroy them. He snatched the remaining grenade and lobbed it at the exiting vehicle.

'Duck!' he screamed.

Both men leapt up and reached the gully they had slept in the night before. Luck was with them once more. The grenade caught the petrol tank of the first armoured vehicle, which exploded and caused a chain-reaction of further explosions behind. Unbelievably, the sound of human voices rose above the ear-splitting noise of high explosive and crashing metal, as a column of armoured vehicles was all but destroyed. Carlisle turned and saw a burning figure struggling to escape from his vehicle. His agonized death cries brought a sneer to both men's faces.

'We'll be back, you bastards,' yelled Carlisle.

'Pete, come on – they'll send the cavalry out any moment now,' said Hardy. He had to drag his mate from the scene, but once free both men moved like greyhounds to escape.

Within minutes they were under the protective canopy of the pines. They both collapsed against the side of the van and took stock of the situation.

'I blew it, Rich. Christ, I blew it . . . lost control. It was the screams. I've screamed like that . . . I . . .'

Carlisle's lip began to tremble as he relived the atrocious memories of the Iranian torture chamber.

'I've pleaded to . . .'

Hardy grabbed Carlisle by the shoulders and shook him roughly.

'Listen! You didn't blow a thing, Pete, except those bastards to hell, where they belong.'

'But it was my fight and I dragged you in.'

'You try and keep me out of a fight,' said Hardy with a sombre grin. 'And anyway, you're not running this show because of any little pips on your shoulder. You're in charge 'cos you're the best. And if you say stand here till hell freezes over then that's the way it is.'

Carlisle's slatey-blue eyes began to fill with tears.

'Oh fuck me, don't start blubbing, Pete. You'll get me going too,' Hardy pleaded.

But it was too late, and the men embraced each other and cried like babies. Then a familiar sound jerked them to attention. It was a helicopter.

'These boys don't hang about,' said Carlisle. Hardy scrambled to the top of a sturdy pine and trained his binoculars on the aircraft.

'He's doing about a two-mile spin anticlockwise and he's low – fucking low.'

'Shit.'

'You could say we're in it,' said Hardy.

Carlisle's brow furrowed as he struggled for an escape plan. Then he snapped, 'I've got it. How long before that bird goes down for more juice?'

'Depends on how much he went up with. Could be ten minutes or could be a long, long time.'

'OK then, we'll wait here for one hour and if he goes down within that time we get our arses down to the shepherd's hut PDQ.'

'They'll have the cavalry out after us before then.'

'I'm banking they won't. We left one hell of a mess back there. They'll have their hands full mopping up for a while.'

'OK then, so what's at the hut?'

'A dead body and a few spare parts, as I remember. We load them on to the Merc and push the whole lot over the edge. It's the only way we'll get the 'copter off our backs.'

'And what if they've got another 'copter?'

'Then we pray to the Lord.'

Within twenty minutes came their third bit of miraculous luck. The helicopter landed for fuel.

'Let's go, Rich,' hissed Carlisle.

The van roared out of the woods, its wheels skidding on the carpet of pine needles, and back down the mountain road. As they cleared the second bend they met, to their astonishment, a foot patrol.

'Go, Rich,' bellowed Carlisle. Hardy's foot had already hit the accelerator and the van ploughed straight into the twenty-strong patrol. Five men died at once and three more leapt to their deaths trying to avoid the vehicle. Carlisle sprayed the remainder and saw at least four drop. In reply three bullets ripped into the van, one just missing them both as it exited through the windscreen.

'Ger-fuckin'-ronimo,' yelled Hardy as they hurtled away from the carnage.

At the hut the body and the remains were already going off. The stench was disgusting but both men ignored it as they packed the van ready for its last journey.

'OK then, we'll take all carry weapons. If this doesn't work we can at least go out with a bang,' said Carlisle.

'Great,' replied Hardy.

They set the van alight and heaved it down the steep mountainside.

'Now let's wait and see,' said Carlisle as they covered themselves with camouflage blankets and began their vigil in the blazing sun.

Within half an hour they heard the deadly drone of the helicopter. Hardy put the binoculars to his eyes and watched it land at the site of the smouldering wreck six hundred feet below.

'Come on, baby, swallow the medicine,' he breathed as the crew leapt out and began to rake cautiously through the remains of the van.

'What's going on?' asked Hardy.

'They're not sure. One of them keeps pointing up and shaking his head. Another one's picked up something. Fuck me, it's an arm. He's waving it at the first one. There's a third bloke who looks in charge. He's digging round now. He's nodding. Could be it, Pete. Yes! He's given the go-home sign.'

As the helicopter took off and headed north to its base Hardy roared, 'We'll be seeing you bastards later. On the road to hell.'

'Amen,' said Carlisle.

They waited until nightfall to make their escape.

'Straight down the road, Pete?'

'Too risky. Any routine patrol could spot us and we'd be dead in the water. We'll head due east until we get to Lake Ohrid. It's about five or six miles across. There should be boats along the water. We'll buy or steal one and get over to Kosovo. Then south to meet up with the lads.'

'What if we can't get a boat?'

'Then we'll swim the bastard. You said you wanted a dip, didn't you?'

'Pete, you're a genius.'

'Maybe,' smiled Carlisle.

Even though their route was mainly downhill, it was long and tiring because of the rough terrain. Both men were exhausted when they reached Lake Ohrid just over a day later.

Along the bleak but beautiful shoreline, about half a mile to the south, was what looked like a fisherman's hut.

'Guess we'll head down there and book a ticket for Kosovo,' said Carlisle. 'Keep your eyes peeled, Rich. We're not out of this yet.'

They walked along the gritty shore of the lake with a rare feeling of comparative ease, the damp air cooling their faces. The enemy was twenty miles away with the shit beaten out of them and they were only five miles from freedom. What could go wrong? As they strolled along they chatted.

'So what do you think of a mercenary's life then, Rich?'

'Well, when you said the pay was five grand a week my eyes went out on stalks. But after the last few days I'm beginning to think I've sold myself cheap.'

'Christ, we haven't even warmed up yet, man,' laughed Carlisle. Both men smiled as they walked along. The thought that within a day or so they'd be reunited with their pals forced all the grief of the last week out of their minds.

At first the hut looked abandoned. Then suddenly a weather-beaten figure appeared and greeted them in Albanian. He had no more than three teeth left in his head and looked at least a hundred years old. Carlisle stepped forward to shake his hand when the old man suddenly leapt back.

'It's the Kalashnikovs, Pete. He thinks we're up to something.'

Carlisle immediately pointed to the rifle slung on Hardy's back and mimed a shooting action, then pretended to eat the imaginary prey.

'*Ah, nier vilodi*,' beamed the old man.

'If that means hunters and not mercenaries I'm with you, pop,' said Hardy.

Carlisle pointed to the line of ancient boats along the shore. He made a few more gestures and it became clear to the old man that they wanted one. The boat they were offered was no better or worse than the others that lined the shore: a wooden rowing boat some sixteen feet long.

'It's not the *Queen Mary*,' Hardy commented.

'And that's not the Atlantic,' answered Carlisle. What Carlisle didn't know was that Hardy, though a strong swimmer, secretly feared the open water. He was dreading this part of the operation but said nothing.

After the haggling most of the notes that the

border guard had given them as change were handed over.

'Good job we kept those. I don't suppose he'd know what dollars are,' said Hardy.

'You'd be surprised,' replied Carlisle.

Seemingly from nowhere a group of fishermen surrounded the old man. Having smelt money, they began to press their own boats on the two strangers. Eventually it was understood that only one boat was needed. This rankled with one fisherman, who slunk off cursing.

'Let's get a bit of rest and then around nightfall we'll go.'

Both men dozed for several hours as the remains of the afternoon light ebbed away. On waking they stretched and let their eyes adjust to the twilight.

'We've been lucky, you know. Bloody lucky,' said Carlisle.

'Yep. If he's up there then he's smiling on us. I'm not complaining.'

'Oh, me neither. It's just . . . well, three incredible strokes of luck and you wonder when the dice will roll the other way.'

'Not until we've got to Salonika and I've been in the sack with the raunchiest whore in Greece, I hope,' said Hardy.

'In that case,' joked Carlisle, 'we haven't got a moment to lose. Let's go.'

They were ready to leave when Carlisle took a last look to the west to check how much daylight was left.

He saw just the glint of the dying sun on metal and yelled to Hardy, 'Cover! Get cover.'

They leapt in opposite directions and Hardy darted behind a large rock just off the shore. Carlisle dived for a similar refuge but slipped and hit his head hard, knocking himself out.

The first shots rang out and cut great gashes out of the boats. But they gave Hardy a marker and he levelled his Kalashnikov and took part of the head off one of the three soldiers closing in on them.

That left two. Hardy made sure that the unconscious Carlisle was not in his line of fire and then waited for the sun to sink lower. As dusk fell he snapped on the image intensifier. The soldiers were inching their way down the last slopes towards the shore. They were not aware that, thanks to Hardy's night sight, they might just as well have been covered in luminous paint. He took aim and blew them both apart.

Then he ran over to his fallen comrade but was startled by another figure darting out from behind a nearby rock. It was the fisherman they had disappointed over the boat. He'd obviously tipped off the soldiers, for he was wearing one of their jackets against the growing cold. Wielding a broad-bladed knife, he ran at Hardy, whose Kalashnikov was six feet away. Too far. Hardy rose, let the thrust come at him and rolled with it. Then he quickly turned his body sideways and scooped the man's arm up by his wrist. The rest was easy. With his knee on the chest and throat of his assailant he prepared to dispatch him, but then stopped. The man's eyes looked up at him not with fear or self-pity. Instead there was a mixture of anger and desperation. This man's crime was poverty. Why should he be killed for that? In his shoes Hardy might well have done the same. He released his murderous grip, and the man rose, stared at Hardy and then walked slowly away.

Hardy turned his attention to Carlisle, who was seriously concussed and could not be revived. It was more than likely that word had spread and that very soon other foot patrols would be descending on the lake. Hardy ditched everything to lighten the load and placed Carlisle in the least leaky of the boats, all of which had suffered damage from the rifle exchanges. But there was nothing for it; he had seen their brand of mercy up at the fortress. And so, using the lights from the town of Ohrid beyond the lake as his compass, he set to, more frightened than he could remember at any time in his life.

The boat was more badly damaged than Hardy had thought and soon began to ship water. To make things worse the wind picked up and before long she was close to sinking. Hardy's frantic efforts to row and bail at the same time were coming to nothing. It seemed he would have to swim and take Carlisle with him. He was deciding what to do when a burst of rifle fire made his mind up for him.

He knew in an instant what must have happened. A foot patrol had found the dead soldiers and then the weapons he had discarded. They were using the night sight, which was telescopic and accurate to nearly two miles. He was a sitting target. Yet most of the rounds missed or tore more holes in the boat. The dice hadn't turned against him just yet. Then a single round tore through the upper part of his left arm. He screamed in pain and dropped to the floor of the sinking boat, which began to slip away from under the two men.

With his injured left arm Hardy clung on to Carlisle and paddled with the other in the direction of the lights to the east. The pain was indescribable. He screamed as each jolt seared through him, cursing his friend in his torment. He swore he'd kill him when they got to safety.

As the combination of pain and exposure racked his failing body he started to hallucinate. Terrible sea monsters reared up at the two men. He could feel hands from beneath the water claw at him as he thrashed in agony ever closer to Ohrid. The world was turning black; there was just darkness bearing down on him now. His left arm gave out. The pain was still appalling. In desperation he grabbed Carlisle's shirt with his teeth and clawed furiously at the water. He was nearly finished and ready to die with his friend when his right leg touched the bottom.

A blind instinct for survival gave him the strength to drag Carlisle the last two hundred yards up the gently sloping shore of the lake. He collapsed on the shingle with Carlisle wrapped like a lover in his arms.

The warm water lapped against their feet all night but they felt nothing. It was just before dawn when Hardy became aware of a figure bending over them. Too exhausted to care, he looked up at the face and stared into the clearest, bluest eyes he had ever seen. They were like two segments of a kingfisher's wing.

'Welcome to Kosovo, gentlemen. My name is Tomarzo. Nicomedes Tomarzo.'

8

Both men were on the brink of death. Carlisle lay in a deep coma and if he prayed to any gods, then only they could save him. Hardy's act of selfless heroism had induced severe body trauma. They were taken to a private clinic in Ohrid.

Lenny Gray had travelled up from Salonika with Tomarzo and was there to greet them. As he was wheeled by, Carlisle looked at rest, almost serene. Gray reached out and took his former major's hand. He squeezed it and whispered words of encouragement close to his ear. Had he known the private hell Carlisle was in as he lay unconscious he might well have put a 9mm barrel to the same ear and pulled the trigger. But he would never know and maybe that was best.

As Carlisle, who had been booked into the clinic under the name of Carpenter, was taken in one direction to be wired up and monitored, another stretcher was wheeled from the opposite end of the reception area. Gray looked down at a desperate-looking creature. He felt a wave of pity to see so young a man in such a terrible state. He turned to the nurse.

'Life just ain't fair, is it?' He didn't wait for a reply but went on, 'Listen, love, there was another bloke came in with Mr Carpenter. I'd like to see him if it's possible.'

'His name, please – the second man?' asked the nurse in polite clipped English.

'Oh yeah. Henry. Richard Henry.'

The nurse's brow furrowed slightly and she paused before looking down at the wasted figure on the stretcher.

'This is Mr Henry,' she said blankly.

'Oh no! No, it can't be.' But it was. Hardy had pushed himself to the brink of death to save his comrade. His will-power had nearly destroyed him. Gray knelt close to Hardy and whispered, 'Come out of it, Rich. Come on, mate. Show these fuckers what 3 Para are made of.' With that he rose and went to find a man he was beginning to hate.

'Oy, Tomarzo! I want a word with you,' he bellowed on spotting him.

Tomarzo was standing outside the clinic, which overlooked the historic town of Ohrid and the brilliant blue lake beyond. As he turned to Gray the early-morning sun played over his handsome features.

'Mr Tomarzo, if you please,' he replied in clear, precise English. He added with a seductive smile, 'Nicomedes, if you prefer. After all, we are friends, are we not?'

'No, as a matter of fact we're not. How come you didn't help get them out? You knew their whereabouts from the border on. You could have pulled them.'

'It is possible, Mr Gray, that I could have "pulled them", as you so charmingly put it. At least at one level, but then alas it would have been quite impossible at another. Not without provoking what I believe your press refer euphemistically to as a "diplomatic incident". And that really wouldn't do, not at the moment.' As he turned to leave the Greek added lightly, 'In any case, they will both live.'

'And what makes you so sure of that? You some fucking medical expert or something?'

'No no, but I am somewhat of an expert in the art of survival. As, I believe, are your friends and indeed your good self, Mr Gray.'

As he said this he brought his face close to Gray's and stared so intensely that the ex-Para felt like he was pinned to the wall behind him.

'You are a gambling man, Mr Gray. Am I correct?'

'Sort of.'

'Then let me suggest a wager. I am a wealthy man but I will stake everything I possess that your two comrades will live.'

'Against what?'

'Against what indeed? Well, Mr Gray, perhaps you would like to make me an offer.'

Gray was planning just that when he realized the obscenity of the proposal. These were his friends.

How could he even dream of betting on their lives. He turned angrily on Tomarzo.

'No offers, mate,' he said with a hint of menace. He didn't like the way everything the man said sounded like a sort of taunt. He was angrier still at having been drawn in so easily.

'Very well. In that case we should return to Salonika and allow your comrades to recuperate in peace.'

'I'm staying here.'

'I'm afraid that is not possible. We have many plans to make and . . .'

'I said I'm staying here!'

Tomarzo was unruffled.

'Mr Gray, please understand I am not inviting you to go to Salonika. I am ordering you.'

It was one thing to be ordered by a man like Carlisle. There were men who counted that as an honour. But to take orders like a dog was another matter. Gray hated it. As if reading his mind, Tomarzo added, 'If taking orders from a complete stranger is too bitter a pill to swallow, Mr Gray, then I suggest you wrap it in a £5000 sugar coating. I believe that is what you are paid per week.'

'Why don't you go in there' – Gray's eyes motioned to the building where his two friends lay dying – 'and remind them what they're earning?'

Without waiting for Tomarzo's response Gray walked back to the clinic to take his leave of his comrades. The nurse was folding Hardy's clothes as he entered the room, and as she tended to his jacket something fell from a pocket and skidded across the shiny floor.

'I'll get it,' called Gray. He retrieved a small button. It was of embossed brass and like nothing he'd ever seen before. The pattern was two parallel zigzags, like the symbol for lightning. He rolled it over in his hand and slipped it in his pocket. The nurse looked at him, puzzled.

'It's nothing, just a little memento,' he said, smiling.

The nurse shrugged and Gray went to bid farewell to Carlisle and Hardy. As he left the building he heard a familiar voice but not one he could place. He stopped and listened more intently, then realized it was Tomarzo's. But it was not the measured, sardonic voice he'd just heard. It sounded agitated, almost hysterical, at times rising to a scream. The effect would have been comic except for what he was screaming about. He was obviously berating the owner of the clinic.

'. . . I don't care about that. I don't have months to spare. Find out what they know now. Fill them with whatever drugs you like. I must know what they saw in there.'

The owner, also speaking in English but with a thick Scandinavian accent, was protesting about the medical dangers. This only enraged Tomarzo more.

'Do you think I care what happens to them after-wards, you fool? They are expendable. Just a pair of guns for hire who ran out of luck.'

Gray could listen to no more. This bastard was planning to put them down like dogs. Two of his best mates. With a self-control he never knew he had, he went to the big Mercedes in the parking bay and waited for his paymaster.

'Everything OK?' he asked as Tomarzo approached.

'Perfectly.'

Just as they were about to pull off Gray cursed and said he'd left a Walkman by one of the beds. Before Tomarzo could say a thing he had sprung from the car and was back in the clinic. He went staight to the owner's office and burst in.

'What's going on?'

'Just this,' said Gray as he lifted the owner from his chair and held him against the wall with his feet six inches from the ground. Gray took his knife and held it to the terrified man's throat. 'If anything, and I mean anything, happens to my friends then I'll be back here with my other mates. And they're not nice like me. Got it?'

Too frightened to speak, the man just nodded his head.

'Just let them rest, they'll be OK. Remember, no drugs. Nothing. Got it?' repeated Gray.

The man's mouth had flopped open and his eyes were beginning to close, yet he still managed to nod meekly as he slid to the floor.

Gray returned to the car smiling broadly.

'Did you find it?'

'Not a trace,' shrugged Gray. 'Reckon someone

lifted it. Still, that's the problem with the world today. You can't trust anyone, can you, Mr Tomarzo?'

The road back to Salonika was rough, dangerous and dirty, and Tomarzo's handling of the Mercedes put their lives even more at risk. Gray was hardly listening to him, for he was tedious at the best of times. You couldn't joke with him and all his comments were probing ones. Gray turned slightly and out popped the missing Walkman from his jacket.

'Well, look at that, it was there all the time.' Tomarzo glanced suspiciously at Gray, who went on, 'All this waiting. Must be taking the edge off me.' Then he put on the headphones and listened to the Smiths droning on about death and the dole. His mind could not let go of the image of Hardy lying on the stretcher. What had they done and seen to end up in that state?

Tomarzo leant over and punched the off switch of the Walkman. 'I think perhaps you are all losing your edge, as you put it. It might be a good idea if you returned to England while your two friends convalesce. You will all be notified immediately.'

'Sounds great to me,' said Gray, who knew precisely what the Greek really meant. They would all return home and a week later the tragic news of Carlisle's and Hardy's death would come through. Then they would receive the coded message 'Christmas cancelled this year' and Tomarzo would hire a new set of mercenaries. And that would be that. Good night Vienna. 'Yep,' he went on, 'sounds dandy. I'll put it to the lads when we get back.'

It was late evening when they reached Salonika and the rest of the team were coming back or going out or just sitting round in the hotel. They were doing anything to kill the slack time before their taste of the action started. When Gray burst into the hotel lobby they seemed to come from all directions and mobbed him. Had he not spoken immediately they would have squeezed the news out of him.

'OK, OK. Just give me space, will you. First thing is they're alive and second thing is' – he paused – 'let's go up and have a beer over this, shall we?' He winked before he went on, 'a little private celebration. 'Cos we're gonna be out of here PDQ. Come on, boys, follow me.'

Shouting and cheering, the three men charged upstairs behind Gray and piled into his room. He slammed the door shut and turned on them.

'Right, now shut up and listen. This is the score. The boss is shot, though he'll get through it no trouble. But Rich is bad. I mean bad. And I smell a rat.'

Gray then gave a full account of the events so far. At the end of his story there was a long silence.

'Well?' asked Pug.

Another uncomfortable silence followed. The awkwardness of their predicament was clear to them all. Then Lane, the ex-SAS man, broke in.

'Look, lads, the worst of all worlds is to stay put. Think it out. We don't trust the bloke who's giving the orders. The real boss is stuck in some hospital bed like Marlon Brando in *The Godfather*, and any minute now we get the heave-ho back home without even a scrap.'

Pug spoke again. 'Point taken on all accounts, Tom, but what's the alternative?'

'Go up to this place Ohrid.'

'What for?' asked Moley Jackson. Big and heavy, his voice sounded like the shape of his body. He went on, 'Lenny just told us the pair of them are out of it. What are we gonna do? Change their beds and cut their toenails?'

'At the risk of sounding pompous . . .' began Lane.

'For fuck's sake just get on with it,' growled Moley.

'Well, OK, it's simply good military sense,' said Lane. 'We might be living the life of Riley down here but this is still technically foreign and maybe hostile territory. The textbook says we regroup round the CO.'

'Except the CO in this case is fucking comatose, mate. Aren't you listening?'

It was Moley again. He didn't like or trust Lane. That made Lane part of a big club, for Moley didn't like or trust many people.

'Before you two girls get to handbags at ten paces I want my twopennyworth,' insisted Gray. 'That doctor reckons weeks, maybe months, before either of them are up again. Pug, you know them both well. What do you reckon?'

'Five days. Six max.'

'Well, let's give it a week. If we don't hear a squeak we'll nose around up there anyway.'

They all agreed and headed for the bars or bed.

Four days later the girl on reception called out to Gray as he was passing.

'There's a call for you, sir.'

'Pete?'

After a brief, crackly pause a voice said quietly but firmly, 'I think so.'

'You bastard, now we've got to cancel the wreaths.'

'I'm sure I said no flowers,' joked Carlisle.

'Save your strength, Pete, we're coming up for you.'

He ran back upstairs and banged on the other men's doors. 'Come on, lads, we're "go".'

It took Moley all of half an hour, roaming the backstreet garages of Salonika, to get a vehicle for the journey. By midday they were rumbling north to prepare battle plans.

'What about the border?' asked Moley. He was at the wheel of the Ford Transit he'd bought for cash an hour earlier.

'No problems,' Gray promised. 'A case of cigs and a bottle of that carpet cleaner they guzzle down here and we'll sail through.'

He was as good as his word. They did. But Moley grumbled on, 'I still don't like it – we've got orders. Tomarzo said . . .'

Gray knew more than the rest and he'd had enough of hearing about Tomarzo.

'Fuck Tomarzo and his orders! We've been told to sit on our arses until his nibs decides we go back home. No one said we couldn't have a little holiday in between. After all, we have come here to watch birds, haven't we?'

'I'm beginning to wonder,' Pug said.

It was dark when they reached Ohrid. A magical full moon glazed the ancient roofs of the old town. The van trundled over the cobbled streets, winding its way to the clinic. They parked and were waiting for Gray to lead the way when a voice rang out.

'Don't move or you're dead men!'

It was Hardy standing behind them in a mock gunslinger's pose. He went to shake Pug by the hand and fainted. They carried him to his bed. The clinic's owner appeared and seemed to bring panic and confusion with him. He hadn't, at first, registered who his nocturnal visitors were.

'Out! Out of the clinic. I call the police,' he shouted.

Then his eyes met Gray's and he went quite still.

'Listen,' Gray explained, 'this a flying visit. We'll just sleep in the van for tonight, see our friends and be off in the morning. OK?'

Four trained killing machines stood staring at the man in a peaceful but somehow ominous formation. All waited patiently for his answer.

'OK,' he said quietly.

All four soldiers were up and ready by six the next morning. Gray led the procession into Carlisle's private ward. Carlisle struggled to rouse himself. Propped up on an elbow, he said, 'Right then, gentlemen, shall we begin at the beginning?'

9

The men seemed uneasy in the stuffy confines of the clinic. Their clothes looked too tight for them, though they weren't. They were bored and confused. Carlisle had seen it all before, and he knew that bored, confused soldiers were tailor-made for body bags.

'Think you chaps would prefer it outside,' observed their injured leader. Even though he felt too ill to move himself, he added, 'Well, come on then, give old grandpa a hand, but make sure you put me in the shade.'

They took breakfast on the veranda and looked down on sleepy Ohrid stretching itself ready for the day's work.

'Beautiful, isn't it?' he said, thinking of the simple lives that unfolded in the streets beneath them. A man in his twenties was kissing his young wife goodbye. A mother picked up her fallen child and comforted her with hugs and a little treat plucked from her pocket. Two pretty teenage girls strode along the sun-dappled road with all the confidence of youth. A taxi passed by and hooted, and the girls tossed their heads angrily in the air. It was a movement that said, 'No chance, mister – we're class.'

The men roared with laughter at this last scene.

'That's us, Pug, that's the brush-off we get,' Gray burst in. 'Fuck me, they're the same all over. And I thought my luck was going to change out here.'

When the ribbing stopped Carlisle continued.

'That's freedom you're looking at and that's what we're here to protect. Freedom. The bastards we're here to take out would destroy a town like Ohrid the same way they'd swat a fly.'

'I don't follow, Pete,' said Moley. 'It's drug runners we're here to knock out. They're not interested in places like Ohrid, are they?'

'That's where you're wrong, old son. They feed like a cancer wherever they are. They suck blood and when they've sucked one place dry they look for another. This town would be a very tempting little morsel for our Albanian drug barons. Life would get more difficult for the people here, and for ordinary people all over the world if it wasn't for the likes of awkward bastards like us.'

'I wish some of the birds out here knew what we were doing for them. Then they might be a bit more grateful,' said Gray.

'I think what you need, Lenny, is a change of tactics,' Carlisle told him. 'But that's the philosophy lecture over for the day. Let's talk battle plans.'

The men sipped strong coffee as Carlisle ran through the recent events, starting from Athens airport. Just then Hardy arrived. He was transformed from the wraith Gray had seen only days earlier.

'Rich, you're a walking fucking miracle, mate,' Gray teased him. 'Look at you – you only look half dead now.'

'Thanks for the encouragement,' answered Hardy.

'Don't mention it, mate. You made a will yet?'

The others laughed at the bullshit and shook Hardy's hand in turn, all delighted to see the return of a warrior.

'So,' resumed Carlisle. 'We were being tagged from the airport onwards.'

'You sure, Pete?' asked Hardy.

'Yep. That woman with the case at the airport. I doubled back while you were in the toilet, and she signalled up at the bloke on the balcony. He turned out to be the second hit man. And the taxi driver that was deaf to the suggestions about his close female relatives, remember?'

'The Clark Gable look-alike? Sure.'

'He spoke English, all right – he just didn't hear a word I said. He was too busy checking his mirror for the trail car.'

Without lecturing them, Carlisle gave a near-perfect insight into the techniques of undercover mercenary work. His account ended at the western shore of Lake Ohrid.

'And there, gentlemen, my life was saved by the heroic deeds of your most valiant comrade here,' he said, gesturing at Hardy.

'Speech!' rang out, and then again, 'Speech!'

'It was nothing,' said Hardy. 'Just an act of super-human endurance, strength and courage.

Carlisle came in again cheerily.

'Precisely. Just another day at the office.'

And there the story ended. There was no mention of the terrors that invaded Carlisle's brain when he listened to the pleading of the tortured men. Nothing about the four hideous days and nights of coma; nor the obscene nightmares peopled by demons from the dark depths of his mind.

He spared them these unpalatable details for two reasons. First, because his body contained not an ounce of self-pity. Secondly, because he knew all too well that fighting men survive on what is life-affirming. The hilarious image of the naked pimp standing in his crocodile-skin shoes was what they wanted. Not a picture of their leader humbled and broken by the expertise of Iranian torturers. Such images were like a virus that could kill that most elusive of organisms, morale.

'Now, tell me what *you* know,' said Carlisle.

Gray took centre stage, thought for a while, then began.

'Right then, Tomarzo collars me one day and says we're going north. Apparently there's been a change of plan. He says you and Rich are on the west side of some lake. Turns out it's that one.' He pointed to Lake Ohrid. 'On the drive up he gets all worked up on the phone and starts yelling at some bloke to "stay put" and "leave them in". From then on he's agitated. He's trying to hide it but I can tell. In the morning we find you pair and tuck you up in your cots.'

'Well, there's nothing we can hang him for so far. It's no crime to expect us to fight our own corner,' said Carlisle.

Hardy was angry. He didn't like the sound of Tomarzo any more than the rest.

'But hang on, Pete,' he said. 'He didn't know how tight our corner was. You don't leave two of your oppos stranded on enemy territory. Not when you can help them.'

'I'm with you on that score, Rich,' Gray replied, 'but hang on, there's more. When we found you I thought he'd be cock a hoop, but no, he stares down like a spider at a fly.'

There was a growing look of menace on Carlisle's face, so unmistakable that Gray stopped for a moment.

'Carry on!' snapped Carlisle.

'Well, this is the bit. He gets hold of the professor in there' – Gray's thumb motioned to the clinic – 'and says he want you two pumped full of some drug. Says he needs information and if he has to kill to get it that's OK. You pair are replaceable.'

Carlisle's fist smashed down on the table. Wood, groceries and glass flew everywhere. Utter silence followed. The murderous look on his face, and his shaking body, made even his hardened comrades fearful. Slowly he regained composure and continued in a calm, quiet voice.

'So Mr Tomarzo thinks we're replaceable. Tell me more about Mr Tomarzo. It might be time to replace *him*.'

There was precious litle to say about the Greek. He had installed the men in a middling hotel and seen to it that they were kept in pocket money.

He had an office on the port side of Salonika and seemed to work there most days. Gray and Pug had seen him from the beach a few times but rarely with anyone else.

'What, no family?' Carlisle said with surprise. 'The Greeks are strong family people. I wonder where Tomarzo keeps his?'

'There's some very tasty birds knock around with him sometimes. But no sign of family, and that's about all we know,' Gray answered.

'Her name's Elsa.'

Every head turned as one to face Lane. 'And there's more – that's if you're interested.'

'Go on,' said Carlisle.

'Well, our friend usually keeps a very strict routine,' Lane continued. 'But I noticed the last three days he hasn't been driving past our hotel at precisely 19.41 like the robot he is. So I thought I'd see where he spends his evenings now.'

'And?'

'There's a big yacht – I mean massive – moored out in the harbour. It's been there since about Tuesday.

Well, that's where he goes along with the lovely Elsa. Though as far as I can see there's no romantic attachment.'

Carlisle had suddenly forgotten his physical condition. He was lapping up this information. There was clearly more to Tomarzo than met the eye.

'What makes you so sure?'

'Quite simple really – he's gay.'

This was a bombshell to them all. But to Carlisle, it was also a vital piece of the jigsaw. The rest were only horrified because they'd actually shaken his hand.

'I thought there was a twinkle in his eye,' said Gray, and the others laughed.

'Don't flatter yourself,' said Carlisle. He'd become weary of forces homophobia. Some of the best soldiers he'd known had been gay. The whole issue smacked of hypocrisy and whatever his men were they were not hypocrites. It angered Carlisle to see them amused by such a cheap jibe. But Gray carried on.

'Watch out, lads, there might be an invitation round to his place for a shish kebab.'

'That's enough, Lenny. I get sick of hearing it. You're in the shit and out of the blue some squaddie saves your life. Do you ask him if he sticks his cock somewhere warm and shitty or somewhere warm and slimey? I wouldn't fancy either for breakfast myself.'

It went quiet. There was no answer to that one.

'Sorry to ruin the party, lads, but it's time to recap 'cos there's something wrong in all this. But, just maybe, I think I know what. As far as I can see, the reason we're here is still good. There's drugs out here, a lot of money and at least one private army. So our original objective still holds. All clear so far?'

The men nodded.

'Two important things remain unanswered, however. One, who is Tomarzo? And two, who tried to bump us off in the Hotel Cotapaxi?'

'And are they linked?' asked Gray.

'One at a time, Lenny. First of all, I don't think we'll ever find out who Tomarzo is, though I'm not sure it really matters. His security clearance puts him above any further enquiry, I'm afraid. It's more a question of what his game is. He certainly thought we might have seen or heard something but that could easily be linked with our shared prime objective. So, as callous as he is, so far he's done nothing really naughty.'

'What? He only wanted us killed, that's all,' roared Hardy.

'Sorry, Rich, but you're wrong. It was information he wanted, not our deaths. Sure, he was happy to let us die, and sure, he's a bastard, but we can't afford to take it personally. Anyway, how many next-door neighbours would be left in the country if you could shoot them just for being bastards.'

'Sorry, mate, you've lost me,' said Hardy.

'Look, someone is up to mischief here and if we plug the wrong man then whoever it is can get another pop at us – only this time they might not miss. Follow?'

'Yeah.'

'Good, then I say forget Tomarzo for the moment.

He obviously needs us badly. Forget the drug barons. If they knew we were on our way they'd have got us on home ground but as it was they positively did not expect us. Check, Rich?'

'Check. We wasted about a hundred of them all told. Lambs to the slaughter. They couldn't have known we were coming.'

'And it's no one back in the UK. If it was then I'd have seen a pattern and there's no pattern here.'

'So?' asked Hardy glumly.

'So I think we get ourselves a berth on the yacht that Tomarzo is so fond of. My guess is the solution's there.'

By the time they had reached this conclusion it was time to eat. The two teenage girls had returned for lunch and as they walked by Gray called out, 'Hey, me and Pug here, we've come to save you.'

They looked up and giggled, then threw back their heads in a way that said 'well, maybe'.

'Long live freedom,' shouted Gray.

10

Carlisle and Hardy discharged themselves from the clinic. They and the other men piled into the Transit and climbed high above the town to laze away the late afternoon.

'We'll sleep up here and be fresh for the drive to Salonika in the morning. Check, lads?' Carlisle said.

'Check, boss,' they chorused.

Carlisle joined Lane, who was staring across Lake Ohrid to the black mass of the Albanian Alps. Without turning to acknowledge Carlisle, he spoke in a sneering sort of way.

'Nice speech that. The thing on freedom.'

'If I didn't believe in it I wouldn't be here.'

'Very noble, and if I wasn't skint I wouldn't be here either.'

'I don't believe that.'

'That's fine by me.'

Carlisle had planned to thank Lane for the work he'd done in Salonika. But he was a difficult man to thank.

'Any ideas on Tomarzo?' he asked instead.

'He seems to like boats.'

'OK, Lane, sorry to have troubled you. Get some sleep, we might be in for a busy time tomorrow.'

Lane made to leave and then turned to Carlisle and paused.

'Sorry, Pete, but freedom touches a nerve with me. You know about my wife of course.'

'I know that she was murdered.'

'Correct, and the animals who butchered her were on bail. The judge apparently said something about human dignity and freedom before he set them free. They went on a little drug binge but that wasn't enough grounds for the police to nick them, so after three hours in the cells they were set free again. The rest is history.'

'I'm truly sorry.'

'Believe it or not I appreciate that, I really do. See you in the morning.'

When Lane had gone Carlisle gazed down on the town. As the lights vanished one by one a feeling of peace nuzzled into him like a fat dog. Beyond, in the mountains, there was a flash of light and a deep rumbling. Was it thunder or HE shells going off? He heard the heavy sigh of a woman from a nearby house. Was she in pain or ecstasy? Carlisle knew enough about freedom to know it brought with it, at times, unpleasant surprises. He'd had a few himself. But if it was the belief in freedom that kept the Khodjas of the world from stamping their paw mark on towns like Ohrid then he'd fight for it.

At the border the exchange of cigarettes and ouzo had become automatic – like a mechanical grab. The border guards slammed the door to their hut as soon as the transaction was made.

'I always appreciate the human touch, don't you, lads?'

Hardy was on the mend as he joked once again with the rest of the men. Moley, who was at the wheel, was about to join in when he hit the brake hard and turned the van violently left then right. There was a loud bang and a crunch as he hit a goat, killing it outright.

'Shit, that's all we need, for Christ's sake, Moley,' Carlisle groaned.

He was about to criticize his sloppy driving when Moley protested, 'He threw the bloody thing in front of me, Pete. I swear. Look, he's running off.'

Moley pointed to a fleeing figure just visible through the dust and mayhem. Carlisle paused, then barked, 'OK lads, out! Out! And carry weapons ready.'

The last of them had left the van and gained what flimsy cover was available when the first rake of machine-gun fire smashed into it. Another burst hit the vehicle and it blew up. In the cover the explosion offered, Carlisle made it to the border post with Pug. Inside the hut the five border guards were flat on the floor.

'Pug, go in. I'll cover you.'

Pug gave his handgun to Carlisle and jumped up at the window, catching hold of the gutter along the flat roof. He lifted his knees to his chest, swung and crashed feet first through the window and landed on the frightened guards. Within seconds the two men had pushed the guards to one end of the border hut.

'English!' bellowed Carlisle.

A swarthy Kosovan guard stepped forward. As he spoke, more machine-gun rounds poured over Carlisle's beleaguered men.

'They come yesterday . . . give money . . .' he said, raising his hands in a gesture that said 'we had no choice'.

A third burst of machine-gun fire ended with a terse scream as someone was hit. Carlisle's jaw tightened and he hissed through his teeth, 'Bastards! Get over there. Quick!'

The guards moved to the windows as they were told. Carlisle turned to Pug and said, 'Cover these fuckers. One wrong move, just waste them. When I'm gone count twenty and order them to concentrate all their fire at the MG nest. Got it?'

'Check.'

Carlisle moved fast in a wide arc away from the border post in an attempt to outflank their attackers. He could hear his own men's handguns spluttering hopelessly against the MG. Unless he could get in close they were finished. At a mental count of fifteen Carlisle was spotted. The machine-gun turned its fire on him and for four and a half seconds he dodged, ran, dived and rolled crucial inches ahead of the murderous fire. He yelled out in his frustration.

'For Christ's sake, Pug! Twenty seconds, you brain-less cunt. Can't you count?'

On cue the five border guards opened up with their Kalashnikovs. The machine-gun turned to lock fire on the border post and Carlisle gained the vital fifty yards with the sound of splintering timber and glass off to his left. The weapon had scored a direct hit on the post but as it turned to fix once again on Carlisle the ex-Para had its operators dead centre in the sights of his CZ.

'Freeze!' he bellowed.

They turned on him and nearly got the machine-gun trained once again on its lethal target. Carlisle had no choice. He opened up and the bodies hopped and sprang in the air as he ripped all three of them apart.

There was bedlam back at the post. Waiting trucks had reversed and hit each other, blocking the Kosovan side of the border. The five guards had stopped the contents of a full heavy machine-gun mag between them and were more or less shredded against the walls of the post. Carlisle checked for his own men.

'Rich . . . Pug . . . Moley . . .'

He hadn't finished before they had all, minus Pug, sprung from their limited cover. Carlisle feared the worst.

'Shit, he's in the border post,' he hissed.

More accurately, Pug was behind the post. He'd anticipated the enemy fire and hopped back out of the window. A machine-gun round had gone through both walls, however and smashed a lump of brick into his face. Blood-spattered and smiling, he looked up at his mates' concerned faces.

'Didn't know you cared so much,' he said with a wry laugh.

Carlisle started to search the area. He'd heard a scream in the confusion and thought there could be a wounded man nearby. Then Gray walked up to him.

'If you're looking for a body it's over there.'

Ten yards from the post was a corpse lying by the wheels of a sheep-laden truck. As Carlisle kicked it over, the fly population of Greece seemed to settle in the exit wound in the man's back. There was room for most of them – the wound was the size of a pumpkin.

Carlisle turned to Gray, who had joined him. They both looked down at the dead man.

'Any ideas?' asked Carlisle.

'That's his truck behind there, the one with the sheep. He came out just after the van went up. I saw him go over to the post and he was waving his arms around and mouthing something. It looked like he was trying to say TV or something.'

Carlisle worked it out in a few seconds.

'TV, eh? He probably thought we were making a film, the poor fucker. That's what it was.'

Gray suddenly looked up and said, 'That's right, he was just wandering around and grinning like it was a party or something.'

Carlisle looked down at the man's simple peasant face smeared with dirt. He bent down and turned it away from the curious onlookers who'd arrived from nowhere.

'Well, he made it. He's a star,' Carlisle said, then looked up at Moley and motioned to the dead man's truck.

'Can you drive this thing?'

Moley nodded.

'Show me,' Carlisle said, then added, 'Come on, boys, we're off.'

As the truck wound along the main road to Salonika Moley turned to Carlisle and asked, 'What we gonna do with the sheep? We can't take them to Salonika – we'd stick out like a sore thumb. You need papers and stuff.'

'We wouldn't even reach Salonika,' said Carlisle.

As he spoke a posse of screaming police cars streaked past them in the opposite direction.

'OK then, I'll give them about ten minutes to reach the border and then another twenty minutes before the helicopter will be out,' he said when it was quiet again. 'Best we swap this. Pull off, Moley.'

They stopped at a Kosovan village where the residents of the graveyard were the only ones not to come out and stare at them.

'Better make this fast or the tom-toms'll soon be going,' Carlisle said. 'That's if they haven't started already. Looks like we've got an audience. Well, let's give them a bit of a show.'

Moley backed the truck slowly up to the tiny village square. He and Gray seemed to be having an argument. As tempers rose no one noticed Carlisle and Lane sneak off in search of a garage.

What they found wouldn't have passed as much of a garage anywhere else but it was the best on offer. And it had two cars standing empty.

Carlisle approached the only person not watching the two crazy foreigners rowing. He assumed the man was the owner and pointed to one of the cars, a neolithic Mercedes with a Turkish number-plate. He mimed driving, but the man just looked at him blankly and walked away.

Carlisle called to him, then reached inside his beige anorak and pulled out a wad of dollars. Three minutes later the Merc's engine was running.

At a signal from Carlisle the men arguing in the square briefly exchanged blows. Lane hit the ground as Gray strode round and let the sheep out of the truck as though in anger. In the confusion that followed six mercenaries and two sheep ended up in the Mercedes, which sped out of the village.

'It'll play havoc with the EC farm subsidies,' said Gray as he placed the two unwanted passengers on the road and watched them scamper panic-stricken in the direction of the village.

They stopped by a run-down area on the port side of Salonika. Behind them was a row of warehouses that were unused, judging by the debris strewn in front.

'Should be safe here,' murmured Moley as he killed the engine. The men got out and stretched after the long, cramped journey.

'Well, there she is,' said Gray. They all stared out across the harbour at the most beautiful boat any of them had ever seen.

'Class, sheer class,' Hardy said with a whistle.

'Money,' Carlisle corrected him, and they returned to the Mercedes to wait for dark.

As night fell it seemed to throw a luminous shadow over the boat that made it look more attractive than ever. People stood on the quayside just to look at her.

'This lot aren't helping our cause. We need to slip out on the quiet,' complained Carlisle.

As he spoke the noise of a powerful car horn suggested that the crowd of sightseers were hindering someone else.

'Duck,' shouted Lane. The irate driver was none other than Tomarzo. He had stopped by a jetty just twenty yards from where they were parked. A huge bodyguard got out and opened the door for a female passenger.

Carlisle's face was pressed to the floor. Only Gray and Hardy could see the proceedings.

'Give me the SP, Rich,' Carlisle called to his oppo.

'There's a woman at the top of the jetty. Very tasty. She's looking out at the boat.'

'That'll be Elsa,' whispered Lane.

'OK the other side. What can you see, Lenny?'

'Big bloke, must be a heavy, he's just standing there and . . . wait, the woman's joined him, whoa, yes, very nice . . . now Tomarzo's griping about something . . . I can't . . . oh yeah, the car's too close to a bollard and he can't reverse. He's giving the big fella more gyp and . . . Jesus Christ Almighty! The big fella's only lifted the back of the car round.'

At this point both men fell silent because the angry noise of a car in fast reverse got louder and louder. It was Tomarzo backing his Mercedes in next to them. Even their breathing stopped.

Tomarzo slammed his door, locked the car and strutted back to the jetty. Then he stopped suddenly and turned, walked slowly back in their direction and then stopped again. His head dropped slightly to one side as though he was focusing on something. With his eyes fixed on the car, he called the bodyguard.

'Get ready, boys. We can't be sure what might happen here,' Carlisle hissed.

The bodyguard was only feet from the Mercedes when the woman called to the two men. The boat out in the harbour was signalling them to hurry. She shouted something again and both men turned and ran to the jetty.

'Whoever owns the boat seems to be an impatient sort of chap,' said Carlisle, wondering where he had seen Elsa before. Her face looked very familiar.

Lane's binoculars scanned every inch of the boat as it rocked gently in the moonlight.

'She's called the *Cassandra*, in case any of you

lads might want to snap her up at auction,' he said drily.

'Crew?' asked Carlisle.

'I calculate twelve. All armed to the teeth.'

'OK then, we'll go as one body and split into two teams. The bow team get aboard, the stern team wait, OK? We busk it once we're on, but remember, these people have so far done nothing. They're not criminals, so softly, softly, catchee monkee.'

They waited a further hour for the possibility of cloud, but none came.

Gray turned to his mate Pug and said, 'What did you make of the big boy?'

'Big all right,' answered Pug. 'Big and slow. Thank God.'

'How would you take him out, then?'

'With an Exocet.'

'Me too,' chimed in Lane.

Such modesty was characteristic of the men. Anyone who had seen Pug in action knew he need fear no one. It was just that he didn't crow about it.

When the hour was up they filed along the quayside a good half mile down the harbour. This would allow them to swim on the blind, starboard side of the yacht and so have the bright moon to their backs.

They swam through the warm, dark water with all eyes on the *Cassandra*. The stroke was a specially adapted one that kept only the nostrils above the water and everything else below. It required extraordinary fitness. As they moved, one close behind the other, across the harbour, they could have been mistaken for a sea serpent. Gray was at the creature's head and Lane at the tail. It was an animal that could sting as well as bite.

The yacht's mooring chain hung down invitingly and Gray had one sinewy hand already in place, preparing to haul himself up when Carlisle tapped him on the shoulder. A single hand movement signalled the drill that he always insisted on. On a visual count of three all six men took a deep breath and held it for a full minute. So expert were they at treading water that not one sound rose from the surface. After thirty seconds their hearing had become acute. But the only noise was the subdued purring of the yacht's engines.

Carlisle gave the signal and Gray scaled the mooring chain. He took his full body weight on his arms alone, to cut out even the slightest scrambling noises. Once aboard he flew across the lower deck and flattened his body against the bulwark. After the customary one minute's wait he signalled to Pug and Moley and the three men went in search of prey.

They weren't looking long. As they crept along the *Cassandra*'s port side a door opened in front of them and the tip of a Beretta automatic came out. From the blind side of the door Gray took hold of the barrel. In one violent jerk he pulled both gun and guard round the door and into the waiting arms of Pug and Moley. Moley's arm encircled the man's neck, while his hand clamped his mouth shut. He lifted him off the floor as

Pug delivered a sharp blow to the diaphragm. Within seconds the guard was unconscious. They bundled him back into the cabin and locked the door. Armed with the Beretta they moved stealthily to the stern. Gray waved the all-clear to Carlisle before he and the other two moved up to the next deck.

It was silent at first but as the men trained their hearing they picked up the sound of two guards pacing back and forth on the front end of the yacht. Gray signalled to Pug to loop round to the stern and back up the starboard side so that they could take both men in one go.

The guards were marching the width of the boat between them, and each time they met in the middle they turned and marched to the edge. Gray gave Pug time to get in position and waited for his victim to appear. The man walked past the bulkhead against which Gray was pinned flat, and leant over the side of the boat. As he straightened Gray knifed him so expertly that he never even called out. Lane caught the automatic pistol in mid-air. Both men turned to see the other guard struggling as Pug's grip tightened on his throat.

Carlisle joined them.

'Good work, lads. Give me that Beretta, Tom.'

Lane handed him the weapon and the whole team mounted the next two decks to the bridge. They burst through the port door and trained their guns on the two astonished crew members. Hardy darted over and took their automatics from them, his eyes roaming over the banks of sophisticated monitors and scanning equipment. Whistling, he turned to Carlisle and said, 'Welcome to the starship *Enterprise*, Captain. Next move?'

'I think we'll beam up the skipper,' Carlisle replied, turning to the nearer crew member. 'Speak English?' The man shrugged.

'I see,' said Carlisle and levelled the handgun to the man's head. 'Now, one more time. Speak English?'

'Yes.'

'It's just amazing how many people learn English with the help of one of these things. Think I'll start a language school or something,' said Carlisle. 'OK, chum, get your skipper up here. Tell him it's urgent.'

The man pressed at what must have been a hot-line button because seconds later the captain appeared. As he panicked and attempted to escape the captain lurched into Pug and bounced the width of the bridge to where Carlisle was standing.

'Don't look so worried, Captain,' said Carlisle quietly. 'Just do as you're told and everything'll be fine. Now, as they used to say in the old films, take me to your leader.'

The captain was visibly trembling as he led the mercenaries from the bridge to meet the owner of the yacht.

The cabin door burst open and Carlisle pushed him through, all the while holding his CZ to the man's head. The men could hardly take in the cabin's sumptuousness. It was about one hundred feet square and dominated by a massive cut-glass chandelier. The carpet was thick enough to lose a dog in and all around the oak-panelled walls were expensive-looking paintings.

The first person Carlisle registered was Elsa, who was by the bar. Wrapped around her slim body was a thin black top and a skirt so short and tight that it was clear there was no room for underwear as well. Her head tilted slightly as she took in the situation. It was that movement that seemed to click a camera shutter in Carlisle's mind. He knew then where he'd seen her before.

Tomarzo was seated on a vast antique Chinese sofa. Standing behind him was the bodyguard and opposite him a man in his sixties. He had a weathered, nut-brown face and greying hair swept neatly back, and was a small man whose build was more sinuous than thin. He showed no alarm as he grinned at the intruders, then said in a drawl straight from the American South, 'Lordy, lordy, what do we have ourselves here? Why, I do believe we have ourselves six real-life pirates on board.' He was still grinning as he shepherded the mercenaries into the room. 'Come forward, gentlemen, don't be shy. Now, unless I'm very much mistaken you all look to me like men who can drink.' He turned to Carlisle and said, 'Am I right in my judgement, sir?'

Carlisle looked away, and settled his eyes on Tomarzo. The Greek sat as still as one of the

Renaissance statues that stood in alcoves around the room. The bodyguard relaxed, and leant on the sofa behind him.

To Carlisle, Tomarzo looked relaxed. Too relaxed. It had to be act. His eyes moved over to the bar, where Elsa swivelled on her chair, her long legs swinging from side to side. She reached for the champagne bucket and poured herself a glass. As she turned again she raised her drink and called casually to Carlisle, 'Cheers, gentlemen. Won't you join us?'

Carlisle sensed a trap and was about to warn his men. Before he had a chance the American broke in.

'Well, that's what I call right decent hospitality. So gentlemen, won't you . . .?'

'Sit down!' barked Carlisle as the man padded towards him, his right hand extended. The American obliged but only after a look of deadly menace had passed over his face. Carlisle noted it and put on his mental file 'dangerous', for the small, dapper figure in front of him. To the whole world he would have passed as a favourite uncle. Carlisle wasn't so easily fooled.

'And your name is?' he said, pointing his gun at the centre of the man's chest.

'You, sir, are addressing George H. Oppenshaff.'

'Am I? And what about you?' The gun moved in Tomarzo's direction. The Greek shot bolt upright in his chair and announced, 'Nicomedes Tomarzo at your service, sir.'

'We've a few things to discuss, Mr Tomarzo,' said

Carlisle. He was trying to remember the hazy details of the figure who had stood over him after his ordeal on Lake Ohrid. They didn't seem to match up with the man in front of him. The voice seemed different. He seemed smaller. Only the eyes were the same. Bluer than any he'd ever seen. Then he continued, 'And time is against . . .'

'Gentlemen,' interrupted Oppenshaff. 'Please allow me. I can't imagine what you have to discuss but I'm sure it's a rather, er, shall we say, pressing matter. Please feel free to use whatever humble accommodation I can afford you.'

He pressed a button on a remote-control device and one of the oak panels slid back. Behind it was a soundproof glass screen that divided the room from a luxurious swimming pool. There were three girls stretched out along the side, each extremely beautiful and each as naked as the day she was born.

Hardy nudged Carlisle in the side and whispered, 'I vote we hang around a bit, boss. No point offending the man.'

'Very noble of you, Rich,' answered Carlisle, who was about to accept the offer, but for reasons of his own, when the door burst open. It was one of the guards they had left unconscious on the deck below. He'd found a loaded automatic somewhere and was pointing it at the back of Carlisle's head.

Oppenshaff, who remained seated, roared at the guard, 'Boy! Drop that weapon.' The guard responded immediately and stood quite still as an ominous silence filled the room.

'Get your ass over here, boy,' Oppenshaff growled. The guard again did as he was told. With the look of a whipped puppy, he crossed the room and stood with his head bowed in front of the old man.

'I'm sorry, sir. I just tried to . . .'

'Shut your mouth. I don't wish to hear what it was you tried to do. You just stand there, boy, and I'll tell you what you just did.'

There was a touch of theatre in Oppenshaff. He stressed certain words for maximum effect but the fact remained that the man before him was genuinely frightened. Oppenshaff was clearly not a man to cross. He drawled on at the guard.

'What you did, boy, was allow our good friends here to overrun the *Cassandra* and it's good luck for us that they are our friends, else you might be looking for a new boss. Do you read me?'

'Yes, sir. It won't happen again,' the guard said meekly.

'You bet your sweet ass it won't. Give me that peashooter you got there.' Oppenshaff took the automatic, stood and raised the barrel to the man's head. The guard must have known that escape was impossible, for he stood dumbly awaiting his fate. Oppenshaff was clearly enjoying himself. A cruel leer had spread over his face. He prodded the side of the man's head and laughed aloud as he flinched.

'Sir,' he called over to Carlisle. 'Sir, as victor of this

little skirmish I place this man's life in your hands. Just one word will send him to the great yacht in the sky. Is it live or die?'

'Let him live,' grunted Carlisle, angry at having been drawn into such a grim charade.

'I guess you just got lucky, boy,' Oppenshaff said to the guard. Then, with a sudden violent swing, he smashed his jaw with the pistol butt. The man collapsed on the ground as Oppenshaff growled, 'But not that lucky. Take him out.'

As the captain, who was still in front of Carlisle, leapt forward to attend to his crew member Oppenshaff shouted at him, 'Not you. I want to see you in my office. Now get.' He signalled for Tomarzo's heavy to remove the luckless guard, and the body was swept up in one powerful movement and carried like a rag doll past Carlisle and his men.

'Like I said, Len, the fella's dead slow,' Pug whispered to Gray.

'So's a rhinoceros, mate, but I wouldn't like to fight one.'

'We'll see,' Pug replied under his breath.

Carlisle's eyes had been fixed on Elsa during most of the incident. The woman had nerve. At the point when it seemed the guard's brains were about to be emptied from his head Carlisle had expected her to turn away. Instead she had calmly sipped champagne. He realized he'd seen Elsa operate in the same cool manner before. She was the woman at the airport. It was she who had waved at the figure on the balcony, signing his and two more death warrants. Not content with that blood on her hands it must have been she who had set up the little trap on the Kosovan border. A third part of the jigsaw was in place. Two questions flashed up in Carlisle's mind. Was Elsa under orders from either of the two bastards in front of him? If not, then who? He was pondering this when Oppenshaff clapped him on the shoulder in an overfamiliar way.

'My offer is still good, Mr . . . hey, I don't even know your name, sir.'

'Carlisle, Peter Carlisle,' he replied, knowing full well that Oppenshaff knew it already.

'Well, Pete, like I said, my offer is still good. So why don't you boys get some dry clothes on and have a drink with us?'

Carlisle nodded.

Oppenshaff fiddled with the remote control again and within seconds an immaculately dressed steward ushered the raiding party to the shower rooms.

As they undressed Hardy turned to Carlisle and said, 'This is how they did the Jews in the war, you know.'

'Bad taste, Rich. Very bad taste. Anyway, our friends out there want us very much alive. Especially the American.'

'What do you make of him?'

'I think we're dealing with about as ruthless a bastard as I've ever met, and if you boys'll make a bit more racket I'm going to slip out and find out more if I can.'

They called in the steward and made some fuss about the shower control. Meanwhile Carlisle slipped out. He'd noted that two portholes on the deck above them had been blacked out and decided to see what they concealed. The yacht was a labyrinth of narrow gangways. He could only estimate that he was in the right area and started trying doors at random. Most opened into sumptuous cabins with four-poster beds. Then he found one that was locked. He raced on to the next door and found that locked too. These were the two cabins he wanted.

As he tried forcing one of the locks there was a commotion along the gangway. It was Tomarzo's bodyguard dragging the yacht's captain along. The man, clearly terrified, pleaded with his captor. For his trouble he was beaten unconscious and, when the bodyguard had unlocked the door, thrown into one of the blacked-out cabins. At that moment one of the guards called out to the bodyguard, and he tramped back down the gangway. The cabin had been left unlocked.

Carlisle knew it was risky but he had to find out what was in there. He opened the door and slid in quietly. The skipper was crumpled on the floor near one of the legs of a vast table that filled almost half the cabin. The drawers were full of maps and tide tables. Nothing that told Carlisle anything. Then, under a pile of letters and other papers, he found a key. The only thing it could unlock in the cabin was an old oak map chest standing against the far wall. The key turned smoothly in the lock and the two heavy doors swung open. Facing him was what Carlisle was after. It was a map of Albania and northern Greece. Salonika was the only part of Greece that was marked. On the Albanian side there were a number of symbols.

There was a large cross at about the place where they had found the fortress. Thirty miles to the north was another cross. Between the two crosses, but still in the mountains, was a small question mark. Finally there were four small black triangles dotted around the same area. Carlisle looked at the map until it burned an image in his brain. Seconds later he was back in the shower room and under the steaming jets with his men.

'Anything, boss?' said Hardy. Lane was at his side.

'Interesting. There are clearly two fortresses. Nearby there are what I assume are four ammo dumps. But there's a question mark that remains a problem. I don't like it.'

'How close to our targets, Pete?' asked Lane.

'Close enough to matter.'

'I don't like this, Pete. And how does Oppenshaff fit into all this?'

'That's what we're going to find out. Come on, get dressed. Unless you fancy a dip in the pool, that is.'

A dip in the pool was exactly what Hardy had in mind and he'd picked the girl he was going to dip into while he was at it. Carlisle noticed the slightly pained look on his face.

'So you do fancy a little swim then? Well, sorry, Rich, but it's pleasure or duty. What's it going to be?'

'Duty, fuck it,' said Hardy.

As they ambled back to the main cabin Carlisle turned to Lane.

'Meant to ask you, Tom, how did you find out that Tomarzo likes the boys?'

'Caught him in the binoculars one starry romantic night. He was out on deck with his boyfriend and well, what can I say? Love blossomed.'

'Wonder where he keeps this boyfriend?'

'Right behind him of course.'

'What? You mean that . . . you mean the bodyguard?'

'Yep.'

The almost ludicrous image of the bodyguard locked in torrid sexual congress with his fussy, mani-cured master tickled Carlisle. He laughed so much he doubled over. When he'd gained control of himself he asked the inevitable question.

'Well, come on, Tom, who packed the fudge? I've got to know.'

'Believe it or not, Tomarzo.'

This was too much for Carlisle. He was creased up again and there were still tears in his eyes as he, Lane and Hardy reached Oppenshaff's lair.

'Welcome, gentlemen,' boomed the American. 'I see my steward has found you slightly more flattering clothes. I must say those other items you were wearing seemed a little out of character with you. Hell, you boys looked like you were just gonna pop out of them.'

'Bird-watching gear,' said Carlisle.

'Is that what soldiers do to relax these days?'

'Sort of.'

'You *are* military men, I believe?'

Carlisle grunted.

'Well,' mused Oppenshaff as if it was of little interest to him.' Won't you gentlemen have a drink with me?'

As he showed them to their club chairs the American fixed Carlisle with his gaze and said, 'Pete, you look like a single-malt sort of fella to me. Am I right?'

'Bushmills.'

'I like a man who knows his drink, sir. And if you drink Bushmills then you know your drink.'

Oppenshaff poured the malt with a glowing look of satisfaction on his face. 'And let me see' – he eyed up the other two men – 'it'll be beers for both of you.'

'Got it in one,' said Hardy.

Oppenshaff liked talking. Not just to hear the sound of his own voice. He spoke largely to provoke. He laid traps for his listeners and watched as they showed wariness or alarm. Each response added another brush stroke to the picture he was painting in his mind.

'You'll pardon me, gentlemen, but I have a terrible weakness,' he said with a flourish of his hand. His terrible weakness was cigars, one of which he took from a box on the bar. 'Now don't tell me these things will kill me 'cos I know it. But then, as my daddy used to say, ain't no point being the healthiest stiff in the graveyard.' He chuckled at his joke between generous puffs on his cigar.

'Ain't that right, Pete? Hell, you know it. Why, in America there's folks that eat nothing but mushrooms. Hell, mushrooms! Can you believe that? There's folks that won't touch milk and then there's some that live off butter on account of some vitamin that prolongs life. Far as I'm concerned they can eat their butter and their mushrooms and sure, leave out the milk, whatever's healthiest. But I'll meet them in the graveyard when the good Lord calls them home.' Oppenshaff spoke as if the good Lord was a close friend of his. He took a long, unhealthy puff on his cigar and turned to the bar. 'Hey Elsa, Nick, come on over here, don't get all shy on me,' he called out.

Tomarzo and Elsa were in intense, almost heated, conversation and didn't hear Oppenshaff.

'Don't interrupt them on our account,' said Carlisle. 'They seem to be discussing something.'

Oppenshaff looked at Carlisle as if he were a creature from another planet. His look said that this was his yacht, and when he called people they came. He turned to the bar once more. This time he bellowed, 'Tomarzo!' Then his voice lowered to a whisper. 'How about showing our guests a little hospitality?'

Tomarzo and Elsa came over and took an empty couch as Oppenshaff shuffled about replenishing the drinks. 'Hell, back home in Charleston – that's North

123

Carolina, boys, a mighty fine state – my daddy would slaughter nothing less than a whole hog to honour our guests. Now that's hospitality.'

Carlisle didn't comment. He'd noticed a couple of things though. First that Oppenshaff had a keen interest in things mortal; in fact he seemed to be a bit of an expert on the subject of death. Secondly, the man had only two ways of communicating. One was in apparently direct yet sly and often subtle questions. This was the meat of his conversation. Then for light relief he'd hold forth as he'd just done. He was getting stuck into his second cigar, so Carlisle took the chance to speak with the other two.

'Mr Tomarzo, as I said earlier, we have a number of things to discuss.'

'We have indeed, Carlisle, but first I must point out we have hardly been introduced.' The Greek extended his hand. His grip was surprisingly firm. As they shook his eyes seemed to pin Carlisle to his chair, and for a split second, Carlisle felt his mind was being read. Yet it clearly wasn't. If it had, then Tomarzo would not have still been smiling. The rest of the introductions were made under Oppenshaff's unblinking eye.

'So now we're all acquainted I guess you guys must be wondering what in hell a country boy from North Carolina is doing all the way out here?'

'I'm sure you have your reasons,' was Carlisle's dry response.

'You bet, Pete. You see I'm a collector. That's my connection with Nick here. Though he's a good deal more – how should I say? – mercenary than I am.'

The comment was meant to tease as usual. Weighing up its effect on the three soldiers of fortune, he went on, 'Not that I wish to criticize a mercenary attitude to life. Hell, if money is all you want in life then that's just fine and dandy by me. There's talk out here of real mercenaries. Sons of bitches are out there killing and looting just for money. How about that?'

'He was taunting them and to Carlisle's annoyance it was getting to the other two. Lane, especially, looked angry.

'I would have thought that all men fight first to stay alive. Self-preservation must come before money,' Carlisle said.

'Now that's a very astute observation, Pete. You're smart. I like that.'

Carlisle ignored the compliment, if that's what it was. 'It makes them very dangerous men,' he added coldly.

The implicit threat was not lost on Oppenshaff, who countered immediately.

'I dare say you're right on that one, Pete, but well, let's not . . .' He tailed off and asked as though it had just occurred to him, 'By the way, where are your buddies?'

'In the pool,' Hardy said, nodding to his right.

'Oh sure. Well, that's just dandy. I expect your friend, er . . .' he broke off and turned to Tomarzo.

'Agron,' said Tomarzo, referring to his bodyguard.

'That's right, Agron. Well, he'll be taking good care of your friends so we needn't worry about them.'

Carlisle knew that Oppenshaff meant that Agron had Moley, Pug and Lenny in his gun sights. Carlisle wasn't going to risk their lives trying to score points in such a ridiculous game of cat and mouse. In any case, he'd sparred enough. He knew all he needed to know about the American.

'I think it's time we showed our hands, Mr Oppenshaff.'

'Call me George. But hey, I was enjoying our little talk there. You're a guy I can relate to, Pete.'

Carlisle was beginning to dislike the man intensely.

But before he could answer, Tomarzo broke in, eager to set the record straight.

'I do believe, Carlisle, that Mr Oppenshaff has shown his hand, as you put it. He is, as he said, a collector.'

'Of what?' asked Lane.

'Things, dear boy, mere things,' said Oppenshaff, whose stony expression warned him not to ask anything else.

'All our paths have crossed merely by chance,' Tomarzo continued. 'My role, as you may appreciate, is as a flexible agent both to your government, Carlisle, and to Mr Oppenshaff personally. The two operations are quite independent.'

'All this is with the benefit of twenty-twenty hind-sight,' said Carlisle, looking at the American. 'But the nature of our task is hazardous, as you might imagine, Mr Oppenshaff.'

'Of course, dear boy,' Oppenshaff replied, waving his hands generously as he spoke.

'And we had to regard as potentially hostile any agents unknown to us.'

'Why? Even a humble collector?' implored the American with mock surprise.

'I'm afraid so,' said Carlisle, though in fact he meant especially so. 'But then in view of the unusual number of visits paid by Mr Tomarzo, we thought . . .'

'It's none of your business, but my visits were mainly recreational, Carlisle. Had you not gone on your little excursion then you and I could have got down to business much earlier.'

Tomarzo was clearly livid at having been under surveillance.

'And you might have spared yourself a bloody nose,' he added.

Carlisle's eyes looked suddenly colder as he spoke.

'At the last count we left over a hundred dead after our little excursion. And myself and Richard Hardy here are very much alive, as you can see. Some blood; some nose – to paraphrase a past president of yours, Mr Oppenshaff.'

He smiled at the American, whose smile in return concealed a mixture of curiosity and respect.

The atmosphere became less oppressive and Carlisle

accepted Oppenshaff's invitation to take a look round the yacht. The others stayed behind while Carlisle went up on deck.

As he stood leaning over the rail of the yacht, looking into the still waters of Salonika harbour, Carlisle felt drained. Turning back to the town, he was reminded of Ohrid. All the lights that moved or just shone out from Salonika spoke of people living their lives, ordinary lives – very far from his.

He smiled as he imagined those townsfolk gazing across the harbour at the *Cassandra*. She must have inspired a thousand dreams. Yet the reality was what? A cold-blooded trio sipping champagne while Carlisle was having to tread as carefully as though he was walking through a snake pit.

A warm breeze blew up from the harbour, carrying with it the scent of jasmine. Warm and soothing, it reminded Carlisle of a woman's body. It occurred to him that Oppenshaff could never have smelt it. It didn't have a price tag.

He wondered how the world turned out people like Oppenshaff, who bought girls to adorn his swimming pool, stewards to serve his food, and who was probably willing to kill for a mysterious 'thing' that Tomarzo would procure for him. Then he stopped wondering. What was the use? The world had always produced its Oppenshaffs and it always would.

He'd had a girlfriend once with mad ideas about everything. One of them was that babies float in the

ether somewhere and swoop down into the wombs of
the people they choose. She'd told him the belief was
Hindu or something. If it was true then he thanked
whatever Hindu god was listening that he had chosen
the womb of a soldier's wife. The naked simplicity
of a soldier's life was the only one he could have
chosen. He felt a surge of warmth and admiration
as he thought of his men; of the hardships they'd
endure, and the courage and humanity they showed
in their own rough and ready way.

Then his thoughts turned down a dark path. Why
should they die when the six of them could waste
the *Cassandra* and her crew? He had all the target
coordinates locked in his head. Ordnance locations
were there too. The mission was safe so what was he
waiting for?

Suddenly the harbour vanished in his mind's eye.
Instead, the hideous image of his friend Mike Greenwood reared up at him. The pathetic sight of a once
proud and valiant soldier so obscenely mutilated
filled Carlisle with a mad desire for revenge. Mike
had died in the service of his country. Someone
had betrayed him. Carlisle was certain of that. The
obvious candidates were at that very moment sipping
champagne in the cabin below him. The question
sprang up once again in his mind. What was he
waiting for?

Troubled thoughts were urging him on and his
hand tightened on his automatic. He was about to
go back downstairs and carry out his lunatic plan

when a tap on his shoulder made him spin round at alarming speed.

'You all right, Pete? You don't look so hot.'

It was Lane. He'd watched Carlisle closely through the afternoon and recognized signs of serious strain. The face that was looking back at his hardly reminded him of his leader. It was twisted and maniacal.

'Steady, Pete,' he said. 'There's too much weight on your shoulders, man.'

As they stood in the fresh night air Carlisle became aware of his own breathing. It sounded like a heavy machine running out of control. Then his pulse started to hammer in his head – harder and harder until it felt as if the top of his skull would blow off. His body started to shake and there was little he could do to stop it.

'Pete, Pete!' Lane shouted, grabbing Carlisle and trying desperately to drag him back from the brink. He shook him violently and as he did so Carlisle's body stiffened until it became rigid. Lane looked into the terrifying abyss of his eyes and realized that only Carlisle could pull himself out of this one. His body was heating up like an electric fire. His skin seemed to burn Lane's hands. The man's motor was on overload. The decision to waste the *Cassandra* had let a demon loose in his mind. Now he had to tame the terrible will to destroy or be destroyed himself.

It was two hours before his temperature began to slide down towards a figure that would still have been critical for an ordinary man; and before the drumming in his head began to falter. Only slowly did he come back from the nightmare he was getting all too used to. Wearily, he thanked Lane for standing by him.

'It was nothing. Don't mention it, Pete,' was all Lane could find to say.

'Well, I still have to thank you. I don't think I'd have pulled through if you hadn't been there.'

'Truth is, I don't think you would have either, mate. What the hell's going on?'

'A mission too far just about sums it up. In my case it's about five missions too far.'

'Jesus Christ, Pete, what the hell makes you carry on?'

'Thing they call extended duty. You know the sort of stuff: checking there's a brew on after the lads get back off a stiff march. Going the extra mile, some people call it.'

'Fuck me, mate, there's more to this than sticking a sodding kettle on. You're gonna crack, Pete. You've got to bale out – now. With or without a parachute.'

Carlisle had never told a soul why he carried on with missions so dangerous that only one in three men usually returned. He looked at Lane's jagged profile as he stared out to sea. Lane was wrapped in his own torment. He'd left the army in pursuit of what he thought would be a civilized life. Instead he'd come home and found the house burgled and his young wife murdered by two crack addicts. With all this on his mind Lane had gone beyond the call of duty in monitoring the *Cassandra* and now he'd pulled Carlisle back from the abyss. If Carlisle owed anyone an explanation it was Lane.

'What I'm going to tell you is classified to the very top,' Carlisle began. 'Understand that, Tom. If you ever repeated a word I'd deny I ever stood here talking to you. OK?'

Lane stared at Carlisle dumbly and in a sort of wonderment.

'Check,' he said finally. Carlisle began his story.

'It was the final assault on Mount Longdon, and 3 Para were in the thick of it, as usual. And my platoon was in it thicker than the rest. We were coming up for thirty-four hours' combat duty. There were lads who hardly knew where they were. Yet if we hadn't pushed for the summit then the sniper and MG nests would have wasted the support platoons. Facing that dilemma, those men were pushed beyond human endurance. When we reached the base of the summit, with only a hundred feet to climb, it was clear to me that some of the lads were delirious. Whatever they did – and for Christ's sake remember this was hand-to-hand fighting – they weren't responsible. I was – I'd forced them to the brink. Only self-preservation got us through.

'Then the MoD bastards turned up and listened to every fucking whinging journalist they could lay their hands on. They had their heads stuffed with weird stories dreamt up by people two miles behind base.

'When the top brass opened an inquiry I could see

the axe about to fall on some of the best men I'd ever fought with. All those men did was to do their duty. But that doesn't sell newspapers, does it. So someone had to take the rap.'

Lane looked at the wasted figure in front of him. So it was Carlisle who'd copped it.

'And where does that leave you now, Pete?'

'Let's say it gives my new masters a certain leverage.'

'And what if you kick back?'

'Then the same kick hits Hardy, Gray, Moley and a lot more men square in the teeth. They only did their duty, Tom. I won't see them thrown to jackals back in the UK. No fat, shit-stirring bastard of a journalist is going to be their judge and jury while I live.'

'They'll come out of it OK.'

'Maybe.' Carlisle stared at the ground. 'Maybe not. But I let them down once, Tom. Whatever happens I won't let them down again. And I mean whatever.'

The stench of Oppenshaff's cigar floated to them along the deck. To escape they walked towards the bow end of the yacht. Carlisle felt like a rock the size of Gibraltar had been lifted off his shoulders. For the first time since Longdon he felt like a free man and it felt good.

'We're going to come out of this one, Tom. All of us.'

Lane didn't share his leader's sudden optimism. He was just glad to see Carlisle back with the sane.

'So what are we up against, Pete?'

'Three murderous psychopaths and two highly trained and fully equipped private armies.'

Lane fell silent, then asked, 'So what's the plan of attack?'

'About a full bottle of Bushmills for me. A dozen or so beers for you and let tomorrow wait. You fit?'

'Try holding me back.'

They strode back along the deck and were just about to enter a lighted hatchway when Carlisle spotted Elsa up on the deck above. His eyes narrowed and he hissed in Lane's ear, 'Keep me covered. This might be our only chance.'

With that he flew up the stairs, trapping the woman at the bow end of the yacht.

Lane followed him and watched as he stalked the length of the deck like a panther. Was he mad? Surely Elsa was just some Greek version of a bimbo. Black hair and shoes instead of bottle-blonde hair and white shoes. He wasn't convinced that Carlisle was in control. Maybe he'd blown it again. Carlisle was close to striking distance now and Lane had an agonizing decision to make. He levelled his pistol, covering the pair of them. If Carlisle attacked then he'd have to wing him.

The distance was critical now and Lane's finger was 'greased' on the trigger. Carlisle stopped behind Elsa, who hadn't heard him or, if she had, didn't care as she idly watched another yacht slide out to the open sea.

Then it became clear that she had heard him because without turning she said softly, 'Feeling better, Mr Carlisle?'

'Explain,' he snapped.

'Oh nothing,' Elsa replied airily. 'I'd noticed you'd gone, that's all.'

'Turn around.'

Elsa turned towards him. Suddenly they were so close that Carlisle felt the dart of warm air from her nostril hit his lower lip.

'Do you want something?' she asked.

From the moment he'd seen her again, downstairs at the bar, he'd wrestled with two violent impulses. One was to execute her for the cold-blooded killer she was. The other was to fuck her brutally. He didn't know which he wanted more.

She did nothing but that was enough. Her breasts rose and fell to the steady rhythm of her breathing; two tantalizing yo-yos he just wanted to reach out and grab. She never once took her eyes from his.

'Well,' she asked again. 'Is there anything you want?'

'No,' said Carlisle flatly.

'In that case, if you'll excuse me,' she said as she made to pass him.

At that moment he pulled out his CZ and held it to her forehead.

'Actually, there might just be something,' he said. As he looked into her eyes he realized a fire had gone

135

from them. Now they were cold and dead and almost sneering at him.

'What?' Elsa asked as she coolly located Lane, who was creeping stealthily closer to them. Carlisle was about to interrogate her when he felt the barrel of Lane's pistol prod the back of his head.

'Steady, Pete. Just calm down, mate. I said calm!'

Carlisle was just that. His hand stiffened on the gun but otherwise his pulse had stabilized and only the icy flame of duty flickered in his eyes.

'Before you do a thing, Tom, move slowly round and get a good look at me. Then tell me if I look off my rocker.'

'Can't do that, Pete.'

'I understand, that's fine, I understand. OK then . . .'

Elsa made as if to speak.

'Shut it!' spat Carlisle, and jabbed her forehead with the CZ's barrel. For the first time her eyes widened and he saw fear dart across them.

'For Christ's sake, Pete, get a grip, man. Just put down the gun. Put it down, otherwise you're giving me no choice.'

Elsa's eyes flashed over Carlisle's shoulder. She saw panic on Lane's face; the man had nearly let his automatic loose on his colleague. She knew that if she could swing things it was now.

'Do it! Do it! He's mad, it's you next. He'll . . .'

'Shut up!' Lane growled. He was on a knife-edge. 'Please, Pete. Please?' he begged.

Carlisle gambled. He straightened his arm out to

full length in the 'execution posture'. This gave Lane, who'd come round to a right angle to him, a clear view of Elsa.

'OK, Tom, if this fails I own up – I'm nuts. If it doesn't then I let go the full mag into this charming young lady's head. Listen carefully.'

Lane listened more carefully than he had ever thought possible. His trigger finger hadn't moved and the barrel was now on Carlisle's throat.

'Go,' he said.

'I'm going to ask our friend here some questions. Watch her, watch her very carefully. You make your own mind up.'

Carlisle took a slow, deep breath.

'Let's start at Athens airport. I think that's where we first met. Am I right?'

Elsa shrugged.

'Oh come on now, so short a memory in a head as beautiful as yours. Let me remind you' – he mimicked her voice – '"Oh please, they're so heavy, a present from my mother."'

Elsa was still unmoved.

'Oh and then you nodded up to some guy on the balcony. You'll be pleased to know you can find his rotting remains in a skip. We topped him . . . sorry, that's slang for . . .'

'You underestimate my English, Mr Carlisle. For "topped" read "execute". Am I correct? But I'm sorry, I still have to tell you I know nothing of the events you refer to.'

This shocked Carlisle. It was his trump card and he'd been sure she'd react. She'd sent two men to their deaths but didn't bat an eyelid. Maybe he was wrong. The concerned look on Lane's face showed he thought so. Carlisle nearly gave up, then he saw the slightest tensing of her hand as he went to speak. He checked himself.

'I'm impressed. But I should remind you that English is a subtle language. Execute is correct as far as it goes, but the method of execution is the thing in this case.'

Her eyes flickered. Carlisle drove the point home.

'They were brave men, the ones you sent, I'll give them that. Would have fathered good stock but we took their genitals first. Christ, did they scream.'

This brought the first shudder through Elsa's exquisite body. Carlisle felt a similar pulse race through his own. There was something darkly and violently sexual in this tussle of wills.

'The one at the airport was the worst. That bastard just didn't know when to lie down. We stripped his fingernails, his eyes, his . . .'

Fat bulbs of water had formed in Elsa's eyes. She didn't blink but they burst anyway, under their own weight. They rolled across her sallow skin and dripped on to her bosom. Carlisle shut up.

'OK, Pete,' said Lane through parched lips. 'You were right. Go on, waste the fucker.'

Carlisle lowered his gun and stepped close to Elsa's shuddering frame.

'Why don't you tell us just what and who you are,' he said. 'And while you're at it you might explain why you've been trying make history of us.'

Elsa led them back to her cabin, where she kicked off her shoes and sat on the bed. Lane found a cabinet and took out a bottle of ouzo. He poured her a glass. She drained it and poured herself another. It was on the fourth glass that she started to sob hysterically. Carlisle, who'd watched her in silence, rubbed her shoulders. She flew at him, punching and scratching and screaming in a language barely familiar to him. His mind raced around the globe, touching on every country he'd ever served in. Then he had it. It should have been obvious.

'You're Albanian!'

Elsa looked up with eyes stained red and black with tears and mascara.

'Yes, I'm Albanian, you bastard Englishmen. And you animals have tortured my countrymen to death.'

She broke down and sobbed into the quilt, then sprang up and hit Carlisle again. He didn't flinch but looked back meekly at her as though deserving of punishment. Elsa's head drooped at the futility of it all. She knew she might as well beat at the hull of the *Cassandra*. After a lull Carlisle spoke.

'I'm afraid we killed your countrymen, yes. But we didn't torture them. They died bravely and in an instant.'

Elsa looked up, half doubting, half hoping.

'You have my word,' said Carlisle tenderly.

Both men looked down at Elsa as she lay on the bed with tears running silently down her face. Carlisle glanced at Lane and nodded at the door. They left her to grieve for her friends.

Outside the door Lane stopped and faced Carlisle.

'I don't know what to say, Pete. I played top dog and blew it.'

His head was bowed slightly in embarrassment.

'I don't know about blowing "it" – it felt more like you were going to blow *me* away.'

Lane's only response was to stare blankly at his leader. After a silence he said, 'I acted like some green squaddie playing cowboys and Indians. Christ! I broke all the rules of engagement, Pete. That's me through.'

He looked up wearily at Carlisle before going on.

'Funny, I never thought things would end like this.' His head bowed again and he handed over his Browning automatic. Carlisle refused to take it.

'Two things, Tom, old son. One, you didn't, and two, there aren't any. Work it out. And keep an eye on Elsa. I'm going to slip down and see how the lads are.'

Carlisle crept along the port side of the yacht until he came to the portholes to the main cabin. Inside he could see Oppenshaff in expansive mood. Pretending to be drunk, he was plying the men with beer and questions. Tomarzo and Agron were by the bar with three young crew members. Carlisle reckoned his absence was good for another twenty minutes at the most.

When he got back to Elsa's cabin Lane was still outside, looking thoughtful. They knocked and entered the cabin. Carlisle poured them each a glass of ouzo less suicidal than those Elsa had dispatched. Then they sat round a low table and Carlisle began to talk.

'We've got a little phrase in England. It goes: "You show me yours and I'll show you mine." Well, I'm going to show you mine, Elsa, or should I say ours, and then we'll see what's what.'

Carlisle told her everything, from the first fateful phone call to the various states of undress he'd just seen in the main cabin. She listened in silence, only now and again betraying surprise. When he'd finished he poured another glass of ouzo and downed it in one.

'Well?' he said.

Elsa gave a deep sigh and began her story.

11

'Mine is a poor country and there are many people who seek to control us,' Elsa began. 'We have enemies within and without. One of each type is seated in the main cabin right now.'

Carlisle was impressed by the candour and clarity of the account that followed. There were none of the traps or innuendoes so loved by Oppenshaff and Tomarzo. The world Elsa described was one where ordinary people wanted no more than basic freedoms. The rest was up to them. Albania had become, however, a dangerous vacuum. Whatever the conditions under the old order there was at least stability, in as much as the shortages and the hardships were as predictable as the seasons.

When the change came it brought with it all the tinsel and trinkets that Albanians had dreamt of for decades. By the second winter farmers and their families would sit and watch ancient episodes of *Dynasty* while their crops and sheep had been sold for the privilege of doing so. Soon, however, the grim spectre of starvation was hovering over them. German stations never got tired of pumping in images of opulence that simple peasants believed would appear by some form of Western magic. Instead they buried their babies and then their old folk, and waited for a new change. It wasn't long in coming to the rural mountains and valleys of eastern Albania.

The first despot to stick his head above the dung hill was the man called Khodja. He was a large, violent man whose origins appeared to be peasant, whereas his links were in fact with the family of the old President. His early followers were selected from the disbanded secret police. They picked clean what was left of the Albanian army's ordnance and headed east to form their power base away from Tirana, the capital. They located a mythical fortress built by the Nazis in the last war.

'Nazis!' Carlisle burst in on Elsa's account. 'You mean the Nazis built that monstrosity we found in the mountains?'

'Of course. You don't think that simple peasants could have put it there, do you?'

'But why? The Nazi sphere of influence was in northern Greece, round Salonika.'

'Yes,' she answered simply.

'That thing must have been built for a definite and one-off purpose. Otherwise they'd have built a chain of them.'

'I'm not sure but . . .'

For the first time since Elsa began, Carlisle detected a lie.

'Look! I came clean about everything,' he protested. 'You know all there is to know about us. I don't know why you're lying, but you are. And that's not cricket.'

Carlisle's language may have sounded genteel, but that was a habit he had when he was extremely angry. His nostrils flared and a bluish vein the thickness of a pencil throbbed in his forehead. Lane saw the warning signals and appealed to Elsa.

'I'm just a simple man. A soldier. If you don't share what you know with us then you might be signing our death warrants. That's not fair. We've told you everything.'

This homespun man appealed to Elsa and for the first time she directed herself to him.

'How can I trust you?'

'Trust us!' exploded Carlisle. 'Girlie, I had a CZ 9mm pointed at your pretty head out there. Do you know what you'd have looked like if I'd let go?'

'I can imagine,' she answered coolly and then grabbed Lane's Browning and slammed it into Carlisle's stomach. 'Don't move. And don't ever call me girlie,' she hissed. Smiling, she flicked back the safety-catch, then added, 'And do you have any idea what your fine body would have looked like if I'd let go?'

Carlisle didn't answer. Instead he looked into Elsa's eyes and saw a flame burning there again. He smiled inwardly because he knew his outburst had been pure jealousy. What was more, he knew that she knew. This secret knowledge aroused him even more.

Lane was picking up the highly charged signals that were racing between them.

'I'm bushed, Pete, can I leave you two to get on with it?'

'Better stay, Tom, just a few things to iron out,' replied Carlisle. He wanted to keep Elsa at bay. At least for the moment.

Then it was back to business.

'I have to ask you again, Elsa, what are you hiding from us?'

She paused and sighed loudly before answering.

'I could be killed for telling you this.'

'You could be killed for not,' countered Carlisle.

She knew that was bluff but her mind was made up anyway. She'd decided to side with them.

'You were right about the fortress being a one-off. What you didn't notice was its unusual shape. Did it not remind you of anything?'

Carlisle's mind shot back to that early morning in the Albanian mountains.

'Only *Star Trek*,' he said.

'Because of the domes, no doubt. Have you not seen them elsewhere?'

Suddenly, to Carlisle, it was as clear as day.

Mosques. The bloody thing was going to be disguised as a mosque! But why?'

'Because it was meant to be forgotten. It was where the Nazis hid their greatest art treasures, stolen from all over Europe. The war was over for them and so they meant to disguise the hiding place as an abandoned mosque.'

'But something went wrong?'

'A prominent Nazi, a man active in northern Greece, moved the treasures to a secret location. When his fellow-Nazis found the treasures gone they abandoned any further work on the fortress.'

'Who took the treasures?'

'A man who became prominent in world politics long after the war ended.'

'And he never returned for his treasure?'

'Not at first – his past would have risen up and torn out his throat. When he eventually returned he found the treasures had been moved.'

'And you know where they are?'

She nodded slowly, then picked up the Browning and held it to her own head.

'Which of you would like to pull the trigger? I'll never tell.'

'We believe you.'

The cabin, though luxurious, had become stuffy. It was highly charged with physical and emotional energy. Elsa opened one of the portholes. The fragrant night air flooded in, bearing the sour smell of Oppenshaff's cigar.

'His smell is on everything he owns.'

'And everything he'd like to own,' added Carlisle, never once taking his eyes from Elsa. Her body movements told him what he'd suspected.

'He wants those art treasures, doesn't he?'

'What he wants and what he gets will be very different things. Those paintings are the finest examples of Byzantine art anywhere on earth and they belong to Albania.'

'In the words of the immortal Oppenshaff,' said Carlisle, 'I say, lordy lordy and amen to that. Anyone for a drink?'

'I'm going to rest,' answered Elsa.

'We'll talk in the morning then,' said Carlisle. Then, as they started to leave, he added, 'I assume you're quite an authority on Byzantine art'

'Yes.'

'Do most art experts look like, well . . .?' Carlisle's eyes were pinned on Elsa's edible torso and legs. The black dress she had on was all but transparent in his own mind.

'Like what?'

'You,' he blurted.

'Perhaps I should wear tweeds.'

'Oh no, don't do that.'

They left and joined the others in the main cabin. Oppenshaff greeted both men like prodigal sons. He stuffed them with caviar and quails' eggs and offered the services of another batch of delectable young women. He never asked where they'd been for the last two hours, which meant he knew.

Carlisle sat with a glass of Bushmills and watched his men at play. Straightforward working lads, he thought. It was good to see them being treated like princes, if only for a night.

'It's a big world out there.'

It was Oppenshaff, come to ruin Carlisle's contentment.

'Was the last time I looked at it.'

'Good boys you got there.'

'Were the last time I looked at them.'

'If a man with my resources and a man with your rare qualities teamed up, especially with these boys, then hell we could take the world by the balls.'

'I'm afraid we only work for governments. And bona fide ones at that.'

Carlisle thought this would be a diplomatic way to end the conversation. But Oppenshaff looked at him as though to say, 'And what the hell do you think you're dealing with here?'

Carlisle excused himself and as he walked wearily to Elsa's cabin he thought, what indeed? He knocked on the door and she answered. She was quite naked and more desirable than he could have ever known.

'Do you want something?' she asked with a patient smile.

'Yes.'

The door closed. Elsa walked to the shower and Carlisle undressed. He joined her and watched the hot jets pummel her olive skin. The water streamed down her body and Carlisle licked it as it washed over her breasts. He let his tongue flick her nipple and it became erect immediately. The water cascaded from her breasts to her stomach and he licked her navel as the soap bubbles foamed around his mouth. He knelt and drove his tongue into her crotch and the lips parted, soaked in her own fluid. He drank like a dog in the desert.

Driving his head hard against her crotch, he scooped her body up against the shower wall. She slid, balanced on his face, up the shower wall until he was at full height and her body weight rested on his mouth.

She hooked her legs round his neck and drove her crotch against his mouth. She held his hair with one hand to push him harder into her and hit him with the other hand if he slacked. He sucked and nipped and licked as she moaned to a climax.

Her body became limp and he lowered her on to him. With his arms straight down by his side he let her rest like that while the hot jets played over both of them. Soon she began to grind against his cock and in that position he carried her to the bed.

As his movement became ever more violent she held his head with both hands and sunk her teeth into his shoulder and neck. He was climaxing as he counted the drops of his blood falling on the white sheet. There were five of them, in the shape of the dots on a die.

12

The *Cassandra*'s launch moved away with a farting noise. Oppenshaff waved to his erstwhile guests as though he would never see them again.

As the harbour drew near, Tomarzo slid up to Carlisle and arranged to meet him the same evening.

'OK,' said Carlisle. 'But the boys have got a taste for the good life. I'll let them go. Might be the last time they see it for a while.'

Morbidly, he reflected that it might be the last time ever but those were the rules and he didn't make them up. He just broke them now and again.

Tomarzo's apartment was as clean and fussy as its owner. Agron led Carlisle in and moments later the Greek joined him. He was tense.

'I suggest the next move is to take a good look at the northern family. The name is Labinot. You'll find him every bit as lethal as Khodja. Worse in fact. Khodja was only after power when the old regime fell. Labinot wants power beyond the frontiers of Albania. And he was the first to start running large consignments of heroin through the country.'

'I'd like to know more about Khodja first,' said Carlisle.

'What for? You know all there is to know. He's a killer.'

'I wouldn't argue with that, but why? Why the ceaseless brutality?'

'Terror, Mr Carlisle. Spread enough of it and people will follow you merely to escape the snap of your muzzle.'

'I assume Labinot's plans are a little more sophisticated?'

'Probably. We know that he's looking outside the heroin market but where is a mystery.'

Carlisle found it difficult to believe that in this part of the world there were any mysteries to Tomarzo.

'No idea what the mystery might be?'

'None whatsoever,' lied the Greek.

'OK then, it's to the north we go,' Carlisle said, and lifted his glass. Then he mapped out the quickest route south.

'Your men, where are they now?'

'Not a clue.'

Tomarzo looked horrified.

'Mr Carlisle . . .'

'Mr Tomarzo. Some are drinking and some whoring. Others are gambling. Just leave them alone and they'll all come home wagging their tails behind them.'

Tomarzo looked puzzled, but before he could ask another stupid question Carlisle went on.

'I don't know quite what you are, Mr Tomarzo, but

my boys are simple fighting men. Tomorrow we go off to fight a dangerous enemy. Not all of us are going to come back. Do you understand what that means?'

Tomarzo nodded meekly.

'I'm afraid you don't, Mr Tomarzo. It means that whatever they do tonight might be the last time they ever do it. Think about that: the last time. For myself I'm going to fuck for the rest of the night so if you'll excuse me I'll be ready for final checks by the morning. Good night.'

Tomarzo gathered up his things as soon as Carlisle had left. He'd noted that Carlisle had mentioned gambling. If any of the men were gambling they were at the Apollo. He was curious to see how good or bad they were, gambling being a passion of his.

The tables were full as usual with most punters seesawing between riches and ruin. At one point of the star-shaped room a big crowd of hard gamblers were standing by the blackjack table. A gasp went up and the croupier looked uneasily at the pit boss, who nodded in an indifferent fashion. A pile of chips the size of the Eiffel tower was passed over.

Gray had just won £26,000 in drachmas. At his side was Pug, whose eyes watched for trouble, not profit.

'That's enough, Len,' he said. 'You've won a fortune. Quit now 'cos your luck's gonna run out soon, mate.'

'No such thing as luck, Pug. The table's in our favour. I just worked it out.'

Lenny's calculations were indeed deadly accurate.

The table had been throwing up combinations of low cards which favoured the bank. He'd struggled through this phase and wasn't going to pack it in now that the favoured high cards were stacked up and ready to flow. Half the punters in the casino had gathered round the blackjack table. Pug was still nervous.

'Come on, Lenny, for Christ's sake,' he pleaded.

But Gray's eyes were like two pinpricks as he waited for the game. He smiled at the big man.

'I'm serious, Pug. I know what's left in the shoe. I've waited fucking years to be in this seat. Watch me go, mate.'

The buzz of excitement had brought the Apollo's owner out of his back office and every eye was on Gray as he called 'card' on a hand of seventeen. The stake was worth £10,000 and the dealer hesitated, not quite believing what he'd just heard.

'Are you sure, sir?' he asked.

The pit boss burst in before there was any chance to answer.

'Give the man a card!' he roared. He was certain the Englishman's concentration had gone. It happened often enough. As the dealer's hand reached for the shoe Gray interrupted the proceedings.

'Wait!' he called.

A look of triumph crossed the pit boss's face. He'd caught his fish. He was about to refuse the cancellation of the bet when Gray called for a doubling of the stake. All around the two mercenaries there were gasps and looks of astonishment. The owner nodded to the pit boss, who passed on the message to the dealer.

'The bet is doubled,' the dealer announced in a trembling voice.

'Card,' said Gray.

The card was dealt. It was a two. The uproar was deafening as the dealer announced Gray's score of nineteen.

Gray looked at the pit boss and grinning from ear to ear, almost whispered the directive.

'Stand.'

The bank's hand was an eight and so any face card would mean a win for Gray. The dealer drew the fateful card as though it was his own death warrant. He turned the card over. King of hearts. Gray had just won £20,000. The owner and the pit boss were quick to congratulate him. The former then turned to the admiring crowd and spoke.

'Ladies and gentlemen, I am delighted to inform you that the young man has won over ten million drachmas.'

Gray just nodded. Still grinning as though he and not Gray had just won the money, the owner went on.

'It is customary to issue a challenge to such a fortunate gambler. I would like to invite you to risk all on the single spin of the roulette wheel. Furthermore we will pay you two to one. Surely this is a bet,' he appealed to the crowd, 'that no gambling man could refuse. Or at least one with nerve.'

Before Pug had a chance to intervene, Gray had leapt in. No one was going to accuse Lenny Gray of lacking nerve. He stacked his chips on the high numbers. Any number between nineteen and thirty-six and he'd scoop a fortune. The ball travelled in its usual hypnotic circle around the lip of the table, with every set of eyes around the table tracking it until it fell. It seemed to slot into thirty-two but bobbled and leapt into twenty-six. Every heart skipped a beat when it bobbled once more and finally nestled into the only green slot on the roulette wheel.

'Zero,' called the croupier. All bets lost to the bank.

'Wait a minute,' growled Pug, pointing to the croupier's hand concealed beneath the table. 'The table's rigged and he rigged it.'

Before anyone could move he turned the massive table over, scattering a small fortune in chips over the floor. But there under the table's lip was the switch used by the croupier.

'Get them out of here,' shouted the pit boss, and all hell broke loose. A gang of heavies appeared from nowhere. They took hold of Gray and Pug and dragged them towards the exit. Then, in an awesome explosion of power, Pug threw the four men holding him in different directions. They flew away from him as though ten thousand volts had gone through them. He grabbed the two remaining thugs holding Lenny and smashed their heads down on the upturned table.

In the mayhem Tomarzo had struggled to escape the brawl by burrowing through the crowd. Pug caught sight of him, dragged him back and held him up like a rag doll.

'You fucker, you're behind all this. Give us our money or I'll strangle you.'

Tomarzo, gripped by the throat, struggled pathetically as Pug shook him again.

'Come on, cough up or . . .'

Pug never finished the sentence. Agron, Tomarzo's Albanian lover, slammed a karate chop on the back of his neck. Pug dropped Tomarzo and stood like a sacrificial bull in the middle of the casino. His eyes were dazed but he refused to drop.

Gray threw himself in front of the next blow and was smashed across the room. This gave Pug just enough time to recover and as Agron closed in on him he let go a pile-driving right hand and stopped the giant in his steps. The Apollo's heavies took their chance, moving in again and dragging the stunned fighters out.

As all this was taking place Carlisle was fighting a fierce battle of his own. Again and again he lunged at the writhing loins of his new lover as the couple locked into a fierce sexual combat.

He felt Elsa's body tense as she approached climax. He withdrew and rammed his mouth against the bruised and battered vagina. He almost attacked it. Biting, licking and sucking until she screamed with pleasure. As she lay back moaning he mounted her again and brought her to another climax. The two of them rolled over and bathed themselves in the tranquillity that only sex can deliver. Carlisle was about to offer up a prayer to the gods of lust when Elsa spoke.

'I want to fight with you.'

'What?'

'I want to go back to my country and fight.'

'Elsa, I don't think you realize how rough it can get out there.'

'You are wrong. I'm no stranger to violence.'

Carlisle looked over the bruises and bites on his body.

'I can believe that,' he said.

'I'm serious, Peter. Had Oppenshaff not arrived and taken all my time up, then I would have greeted you at the Hotel Cotapaxi.

The meaning of Elsa's remark wasn't lost on Carlisle.

'I assume you mean you would have killed me.'

'Exactly. I would kill any enemies of my country. We were told that you were going into the mountains and we assumed you intended to steal the icons.'

'You assumed!' Carlisle was livid. 'You assumed and that assumption cost eight innocent men their lives. The poor bastard who owned the Cotapaxi, the stupid truck driver on the border, as well as your own men. They needn't have died and you can't bring them back.'

Carlisle was about to accuse Elsa of playing God when she spoke again.

'I wish I could bring them back. One of them was my brother.'

Carlisle was struck dumb.

'Oh God,' he mumbled. 'I . . . if I'd known.'

'There is no way you could have known. He died knowing the risks. He was a brave boy.'

Carlisle couldn't hear or feel anything but he knew that Elsa was crying bitterly as she lay next to him. The two of them stared out of her apartment window. The moon was high in a clear sky.

'Someone is going to pay for your brother's death, Elsa. Leave it to me. I give you my word.'

Back at the hotel Moley rolled off the fat Greek prostitute he'd paid for an hour earlier. He thanked her though it was obvious she understood no English, gave her the ten thousand drachmas and added a thousand as a tip. She took the money with no comment. They parted at the door in total silence.

Hardy was lying awake in his bed. His mind was back in Newcastle. He was in a pub called the Crown Posada with a girl called Celia. She was a mad, beautiful girl who'd come from nowhere and changed his life. She'd been to university and played the flute. She dressed in weird clothes and gave him sex so wild he thought he'd die of pleasure. He'd never known anything like her and now she was telling him it was all over. The pain he suffered was beyond anything he thought possible. Maybe, just maybe when he got home loaded with money, he could buy a flat. Maybe he could get a car and they could just drive away and say fuck it to the world. Maybe.

Pug and Gray had found a friendly bar and drank the rest of the night away.

'I nailed the fucker,' roared Pug.

'In one,' chortled his mate.

It didn't matter to either man that no one else in the bar understood a word of English. They'd come out of another scrape together and tomorrow they'd do the same. They drank until they could barely stand.

Lane was restless and took a walk down by the dock. The *Cassandra* looked like a floating wedding cake out in the harbour. He knew that she was a beautiful sight but his mind had become numb to the beautiful things in life. Carlisle's call had, at least temporarily, saved him from self-destruction. But he knew in his heart that his life had no purpose any more. He might have wondered where on the yacht was the gorgeous girl he had bedded twenty-four hours earlier. Instead his mind had gone down the same dark tunnel. To the trial of his wife's murderers. He could still hear the silky voice of the defence barrister pleading with the gullible jury. He could still see the shock on their faces as the previous convictions for violence and attempted rape were read out. The smirks up to the public gallery as the plea of diminished responsibility was accepted. In two or three years they would be out. Lane only wanted to live long enough to meet up with them again. Albania held no terrors for him. Nothing would destroy Thomas Lane before his final act of vengeance. Nothing.

He lifted his high-power binoculars and took one last look at the *Cassandra*. There was some activity on the lower deck. Two crew members had hold of the luckless skipper. Oppenshaff, easily recognizable with his silvery hair flying about, was laying into the captive with his pistol butt. When the skipper was dropped unconscious to the deck the American held the gun to his head and pulled the trigger. Even in the dim half light Lane could see the man's brains spray up into his killer's face. Oppenshaff walked off without even wiping away the mess.

That was the men's last night in Salonika. None of them could have dreamt of the incredible events that were about to unfold. But then none of them would have wanted to know.

13

Tomarzo had spent the night in deep concentration. He had a problem. He had assumed that the mercenaries would be dim but efficient. But these men were not so easily fooled.

Probably they knew already that there was a huge quantity of heroin in the mountains. They might even know about the deal with Oppenshaff. Just this knowledge would make them dangerous to Tomarzo. But if they'd found out the figure the American would pay for the Byzantine pieces, then they could well be deadly.

Yet they were the only force capable of removing Khodja and Labinot. There was no chance of tracking down the art treasures until the two Albanians were taken out of the equation. Tomarzo was no soldier but he knew that Carlisle's men were highly professional killers. He decided the only plan was to send them in and worry about the Oppenshaff connection after. He had just reached this conclusion when the doorbell sounded. The time was eight exactly.

161

'Welcome, gentlemen, I appreciate punctuality,' said Tomarzo as he opened the door.

'Good,' answered Carlisle, who didn't give a damn what Tomarzo appreciated. 'OK then, lads, get yourselves sat down. We're about to get a lesson in the art of war.'

The Greek produced the same map that Carlisle had seen onboard the *Cassandra*. There were two changes, however. Two ammo dumps were shown on Tomarzo's map instead of three. And the mysterious question mark had been removed.

'Here, gentlemen, is all the information you will need,' the Greek said. 'The objective is clear: to destroy the mountain strongholds of both Khodja and Labinot.'

'How?' asked Carlisle slyly.

'I . . . well, I . . .' Tomarzo was flustered. He was a fixer, not a fighter.

Carlisle rose and put him out of his misery.

'Don't worry, Mr Tomarzo,' he said, snatching the map and other data from the Greek,' we'll take care of the dirty stuff. You just stay her and keep Oppenshaff company. I'm sure the two of you have a great deal to discuss. Especially with us out of the way.' He studied the eager faces of his men.

'Ready, boys? OK, then let's go. We've got some fighting to do.'

As they filed out Pug leant close to Tomarzo.

'We want that money, mate. And we'll be back for it. Don't worry about that.'

Hardy sidled up to Carlisle as they left the apartment and walked back to the hotel.

'Bit hasty back there, Pete. He might have had some useful info. This is his neck of the woods when all's said and done.'

Carlisle looked Hardy square in the eye but didn't utter a single word. His look said it all.

'Point taken, boss,' answered Hardy.

When they got back to the hotel Carlisle ordered coffee and they sat in his room for the final briefing.

'Before we start, young Rich here thought I was a bit hard on our friend earlier. Let me give you the low-down on Tomarzo. Basically he's a lowly piece of scum working for us and Oppenshaff at the same time. What neither of them knows is that I've seen the original of this.' Carlisle held up the map and filled in the missing ammo dump and the question mark as accurately as he could recall.

'So, what's he playing at?' asked Lane.

'I don't fully know, but our position is still clear. As long as Khodja and Labinot are running the show, Albania remains unstable. We're paid up to the moment they're eliminated. After that, or so the theory goes, we return home and take up our jobs in the building society again.'

'That's the theory, but what have you got in mind, Pete?' asked Hardy.

'Well, let's fight one battle at a time, but assuming none of us heads for the great barracks in the sky, we let the dust settle. Once the all-clear sounds then

I vote we do a bit of nosing around on our own account.'

This last proposal was met with grunts of approval. Though Carlisle rarely showed it, he was never happier than in the final battle prep. The feeling was like the last moment before sex. The deep pleasure of knowing that every second of your life had led to this single point. The point of no turning back. And here, sharing the experience, were five of the finest fighting men for hire anywhere in the world. Fear and self-doubt were burned alive in the furnace of such emotions.

'What's their strength, Pete?' Hardy spoke for all of them.

'About a thousand men in either camp. They've got at least one heavy artillery piece each and general transport. Personal weapons appear to be the latest and there's at least one 'copter around. They've got local knowledge and apparently impregnable defences. That's about it, lads.'

Hardy and Lane whistled almost in unison. The ex-SAS man asked the obvious question.

'What about their weaknesses? Have they got any?'

'They certainly have, Tom. Us!'

Gray couldn't resist jumping in:

'Oh well then, what chance have they got?'

But Carlisle's head was spinning with the strong black coffee and the intense feeling of camaraderie. He had no reservations.

'If we fight the way we can and if each man looks out for the other, they haven't got a snowball in hell's chance.'

No one doubted Carlisle, not when he was in this mood. He went on.

'I think it's safe to say that our cover as ornithologists has been blown. We'll be in standard desert light issue from here on in. We'll travel by foot and by night. ETA on the first ammo dump will be 0600 hours on the twenty-fourth. That's two and a half days away. So get some grub down your necks. We'll take minimum carry weapons and light compo. Any questions?'

Predictably there were none.

Before they set off Carlisle paid Tomarzo a final visit. The Greek was sitting in his office thinking. The gigantic figure of Agron blotted out most of the window. The thin shaft of light that squeezed past the huge Albanian lit Tomarzo's angry face.

'I'll thank you for a little more respect in future, Mr Carlisle,' he snapped. 'Perhaps I should remind you, I am your superior.'

'So I gather,' answered Carlisle with a wry smile. 'And I'm sure that as my superior you won't allow anyone to tail us to the border.'

'Why should anyone tail you to the border?'

'Now that's a very good question. I personally can't imagine why. It's just that various people have expressed great curiosity about us since we arrived.' Carlisle was still smiling but then his expression changed abruptly. 'For the record, we've killed all of them. And if we are followed again then we'll start playing really rough. Got it?'

'I think we understand each other, Mr Carlisle,' said Tomarzo as he rose and offered his hand to Carlisle. 'May I take the opportunity to wish you good luck and Godspeed.' Carlisle ignored his hand.

'We'll be in touch,' he said as he walked to the door.

An hour later the six men were heading north in the battered Mercedes saloon with the Turkish number-plates. They'd eaten at two and then cleared the hotel of even the slightest trace of evidence that they'd ever been there. By evening the car pulled up, rattling and banging, in what looked like the middle of nowhere.

'Where are we?' asked Gray.

'In the middle of nowhere, I hope,' said Carlisle coolly. Then, in response to the puzzled looks from both Gray and Pug, he added, 'Because nowhere is a difficult place to find. And we don't want to be found.'

'Just for the record, boss. Which way's somewhere?' asked Gray.

'The way we came,' Carlisle said, jerking his thumb over his shoulder. 'And that's where we're heading,' he added, nodding in the opposite direction. 'Albania.'

The ground dropped away in front of them into a dried-up river-bed.

'Moley, hide the wagon down there and cover it with what brush you can find. Give him a hand, some of you. We'll rest up till nightfall,' said Carlisle briskly.

As they sat in the shallow gully Carlisle issued further instructions.

'Tom, take the compass and charts and keep to the middle of the column. Rich, you lead. No one, and I mean no one, will even dream of using an image intensifier. They fuck your night vision to bits. By the time we get up north I expect you lot to have eyes like bushbabies. Got it?'

They chorused expletives and waited for night to descend. The final scarlet bead of sun dropped out of the western sky. Then, under a nearly full moon, they set off.

It wasn't long before they had reached high ground. The terrain was rough and taxing. By midnight they'd covered ten miles and took a rest near a pine wood.

'The first ammo dump is north-west of here,' said Carlisle. 'If we keep to this side of the mountains we can't go wrong. Let's take a breather.'

As he gave the order he noticed Hardy peering into the trees, his head cocked.

'Everything OK, Rich?'

'Could be my imagination, but I think we're being tailed.'

'Check,' replied Carlisle. 'Someone's been about since we hit the high ground.'

'Any ideas?'

'Search me. We'll fake a move-out and double back. Let's just slot the fucker.'

They stayed for another five minutes and dropped to lower ground out of sight of their stalker. Then Carlisle and Hardy ran a quarter of a mile in a circle, to trap their victim from behind. They caught sight of him as they closed but somehow when they went in for the kill he'd lost them.

Hardy couldn't believe it. He and Carlisle had pulled the same trick a dozen times against well-trained soldiers. It had never failed.

'What now, Pete?' Hardy whispered.

'The fucker's in this wood and he's got to be close. Let's wait and see.' They remained under cover but whoever had tailed them was staying put too. After an hour they rejoined the others.

'Listen, lads, we've got a tail and he's good. He's slipped me and Rich, so the only thing is to get some steam up. Come on, we'll march the legs off the bastard.'

They set out on a forced march that took them thirty-two miles in just under four hours. The sun was rising as they reached a craggy overhang.

'Get tight in here, lads. We'll eat and then rest up through the day. Anyway, looks like we lost our tail. Don't know who Tomarzo sent after us but he'd have had to have been a mountain goat to keep up with that tab.'

Carlisle had spoken too early. As they wedged

themselves tight into the mountainside a figure slipped up on to the high ground above them. From there they were watched for the rest of the day.

The cooling air woke Carlisle and his men. They roused themselves and were about to eat when Carlisle turned suddenly.

'Where's Rich, for fuck's sake?'

Hardy had vanished. In fact as Carlisle was speaking he was homing in on his target. He'd slipped out at nightfall and tracked up the mountain to the high ground he would have taken if he was tailing. As he worked cautiously down the mountain he saw the stalker lifting himself from a hollow.

Brilliant cover, thought Hardy. But not quite brilliant enough. He was no more than twenty yards from his prey and closed the gap at incredible speed. His arm locked round the man's neck and snapped his head back. He was about to dispatch him when the largest, most beautiful eyes he'd seen stared back at him defiantly. They were Elsa's.

Carlisle was furious when he saw Hardy approaching silently with the woman, her hands tied.

'Steady, Pete, there's no real harm done,' urged Hardy.

'No real harm? Who's going to escort her back to Greece? Do you realize how much time we could lose. And we haven't got bloody time. The woman is a liability.'

'Thing is, Pete, no one escorted her here, so why

169

does she have to be wet-nursed all of a sudden?' asked Lane.

The real reason for Carlisle's anger was his concern for Elsa. Hardy might have cut her throat. He couldn't bear the thought of any harm coming to her.

'Shut your mouth, Lane! he exploded again. 'You!' He pointed at Elsa. 'You're a liability. Get back to your cosy life in Salonika, girlie, and . . .'

Before Carlisle could finish, Elsa had grabbed Lane's automatic and released the safety-catch. The barrel was between his eyes.

'I told you before never to call me that. This morning I could have slit your throats where you slept. I moved around you as you snored your English heads off.'

'And what does all that mean, girlie?'

Elsa's eyes burned bright at this second jibe from Carlisle.

'It means I'm every bit as good a soldier as anyone here. It means that I will fight for my country by your side or waste you where you stand. Now I demand a vote.'

Carlisle's eyes moved questioningly over the taut faces of his men. Their faces said yes to a man. He didn't bother to ask.

'You are duly elected as an honorary member of the dirty half dozen by five votes to one. Now, could I please have the gun?'

Elsa handed the automatic to Carlisle. He took the

gun and then threw a lethal right hand cross at Elsa, knocking her flat. He stood over her as she looked up amazed at him.

'Any one of the lads here would have guessed that punch was on the way. Take a tip from the Boy Scouts, my girl. Always be prepared.'

Gray and Pug helped Elsa to her feet. They wiped the blood from her nose and Gray said with a gigantic grin on his face, 'Welcome to the club.'

'Thanks, Lenny,' she replied. 'After a punch like that I hope it's life membership.'

Carlisle had heard this and said darkly, 'Depends how long your life lasts.'

They moved away after compass directions and bearing had been finalized. The country didn't get any easier but they had clearly got into Albania undetected, as no further incident followed. The waning moon offered just enough light and they made good progress. By morning they'd covered another twenty miles. The first ammo dump was within reach.

They took cover in one of the many pine woods that softened the lowest slopes of the mountains. In the dark Elsa moved closer to Carlisle. She could smell the mixing of the pine needles with his musky, almost sour odour. He in turn could smell her sweet breath as they moved even closer and kissed. Her hand moved in wild, searching movements over his body. Even though it was clothed he became fired by her sensuous probing. She slid her hand into his trousers and rubbed his aching cock. Her hand moved lower and she grabbed his balls like a vice.

Carlisle managed not to shriek out loud but the pain was intense.

'What was that about the Boy Scouts, Peter? Always be prepared?'

He was passing out with the pain when she let his balls go.

'Now come into me,' she whispered imperiously. Carlisle did as she said. It was not possible to do anything else.

Hardy got his hexamine stove going and in the fading light of the evening made a brew with water from the spring he had found. The rest slowly roused themselves and uncoiled from their slumbers. Elsa grabbed a towel and headed for the spring.

'Tea up, lads,' Hardy called. Pug was the first to offer up his battered tin mug. As he did he commented with a gleam in his eye, 'I heard a funny old rumpus earlier. What about you, Rich?'

'Matter of fact, I did hear something, Pug. Yeah, a sort of panting and yelping.'

The rest chimed in about the terrible animal noises they had heard. Carlisle roused himself and joined the rest. By now the talk was of wolves.

'Did you hear them, Pete?'

'Hear what?'

'Well, Pug and the rest reckon there were wolves prowling about.'

'Can't say I did, lads,' he answered innocently,

but he knew exactly what they were talking about. 'Shouldn't worry, though, there's a lot of myths about wolves. They're actually quite timid creatures.' Carlisle grinned to himself, knowing he was in for some stick.

'The one I heard didn't sound very timid,' joked Gray. 'Sounded like a she-wolf. She had something by the neck, I reckon, 'cos there was this fierce panting and . . .'

'OK, Lenny, thanks for the hint. We'll bed down at a respectable distance in future.'

'Bed down? Don't follow you, boss. We were just discussing the wolves up here in the mountains and . . .'

'All right,' grinned Carlisle. 'I give in. I'm going for a wash. See you in ten minutes.'

'Watch out for the she-wolf, Pete,' said Gray, still deadpan. 'She's got your scent, mate.'

The rest called after him with similar wisecracks. Their voices were just fading as he spotted Elsa by the spring. He watched her from the cover of a pine. She was stripped to the waist, her breasts jutting out provocatively. The nipples were erect in the cool evening air. Carlisle felt his cock stiffen to breaking point. He was almost frightened of the lust this woman ignited in him.

Elsa dried her upper body and loosened her trousers before letting them fall around her ankles. She bent nearer the spring and so raised her rear up in Carlisle's direction. He was reaching a frenzy.

She could hear him panting now and smiled to herself.

'Well,' she said as she turned to him, 'what are you waiting for?'

They joined the rest of the lads, who were ready to go. With a look that defied any further banter, Carlisle simply said, 'Gentlemen, shall we get on our way? I believe we have a battle to fight.'

14

The night was cloudy and they made slow headway in the poor light. There were stumbles and falls but no one complained. Around three in the morning Carlisle ordered a halt.

'Tom, could you come back here a minute,' he called to Lane. Carlisle was seated looking up at a high mountain peak off to the east as the man filtered back through the column.

'That could be our baby. What do the charts show?'

'Looks promising, Pete. The compass bearing's good and the notes on the local features all tie in.' Lane looked up at the same peak Carlisle was studying. 'Does that remind you of a tomahawk?' he asked.

'Sort of, with a chip out . . .' replied Carlisle.

Lane finished the sentence.

'Out of the top-right corner,' he said. 'Then that's definitely our baby. OK then, according to the rest of the details the ammo dump is somewhere within four hundred metres of here.'

'The question is, where? What do the notes say?'

'Nothing. They only describe the surrounding area.'

'Great. Still, it's here somewhere. What's your guess?'

Lane's eyes moved over the rugged features all about them. They were in a sort of shallow valley. The mountain rose steeply to their right and levelled to the left. Ahead of them the track rose gradually until it reached a pine wood. Just on the edge of this Lane spotted a small building, and he pointed it out to Carlisle.

'Let's go for it,' said Carlisle. 'I don't see a better candidate.'

The building turned out to be a deserted shepherd's hut. It was completely empty. The trees behind the hut formed a black wall.

'Good cover if nothing else,' said Carlisle. 'We'll rest up here and check things over in the morning.'

They bedded down just inside the wood and slept like the dead. Carlisle was woken with the prodding of a Kalashnikov at his throat.

'Oh Grandpapa, what big eyes you have,' said Elsa, laughing.

'Where the hell did that come from?' Carlisle's startled eyes were fixed on the rifle she was holding. Elsa turned it round and placed it carefully beside him.

'You've been sleeping on it and a hundred more all night. Come with me.'

They walked to the far end of the hut, where Elsa bent and lifted a heavy flagstone.

'There's a short drop and then a tunnel leads to the dump. It's built under the woods.'

'Who the hell dug this thing out?'

'I don't know. They're all over the mountains. The partisans adapted them in the war.'

Carlisle called the rest of the men and they crawled along to the main chamber. In the ghostly torchlight they examined the cache of weapons.

'Moley, what's the score on HE?'

'Got enough to blow up Albania, let alone Laminated Top, or whatever his name is.'

Elsa had thrown Moley a dirty look.

'Not that we'd want to blow up Albania,' he added. He and the other men had developed a healthy respect for the raven-haired beauty.

All the essential equipment was dragged out of the dump. Grenades, high explosive and mines were checked over. A heat-seeking launcher was assembled and magazines counted.

'All in all a useful little stash,' said Carlisle, relieved. He hadn't liked taking Tomarzo at his word. But now morale was sky-high. With the exception of Lane.

'OK, Tom?' asked Carlisle.

'Yeah, fine.'

But he wasn't and it showed.

'Spit it out,' insisted Carlisle.

'I don't want to spoil the party but this lot would be fine against an outfit like ourselves – you know, one on the hoof. But what are we going to do against a small army with heavy fortifications?'

None of the others had thought to ask. They had served under Carlisle before, and their confidence in him was absolute.

'Fair question,' said Carlisle as he leant back against a pine and watched his men already loading up for another gruelling tab. 'To put it simply, I've got a hunch. And my hunches are usually good.'

'Go on.'

'Well, I'm a simple country boy at heart. Grew up next to a farm. And know what? It was never two cockerels in the barnyard. Simple reason: there's only room for one. Got me?'

Lane's keen mind had grasped it in one.

'So how long before Khodja and Labinot go for each other's throats?' he asked.

Carlisle grinned broadly. He was pleased to see Lane's mind was on the job.

'As soon as we give them reason to. First though, I think we'd better take a look and see where Mr Labinot hangs his hat. It might tell us a lot.'

Under the increased weight of arms they moved slowly north-east towards Labinot's stronghold. Two days later they were within earshot of their destination. Sporadic rounds of small-arms fire and the deep rumble of artillery shells told them that the drug baron's private army was in training.

It was just after dusk when the team took up their observation posts. They were high above the stone fortress that had been built partly into the mountainside. The walls were about ten feet thick and nearly twice as high. The perimeter wall formed about half a square mile and contained a parade ground of sand.

'Who built this thing in the first place?' Carlisle asked Elsa.

'Would you remember if I told you?'

'Probably not. But I need to know how deep into the mountain it goes.'

'These were the strongholds of mountain kingdoms. The excavations would have been very thorough.'

'I was afraid of that.' Carlisle paused and seemed lost in thought. 'Then we'll have to draw the hornet out of his nest.'

'When?' asked Elsa, eager for the fight.

'Softly, softly, catchee monkee. Let's see what our monkey gets up to in his spare time.'

In the morning the predictable routines of an army garrison were acted out. Lane had his binoculars trained on the fort the whole day. There was nothing but routine until the sound of a large truck off in the distance appeared to create a flurry of activity inside the fort.

'Something big on the way, Pete. Lot of excitement down there,' said Lane.

A massive truck growled and snarled its way up from the southerly approach to the fort.

'Looks like a grub wagon – it's refrigerated,' said Lane. Carlisle grabbed the binoculars.

'Don't think it's a leg of lamb that's getting them so worked up down there,' he said, and as he spoke

179

the truck pulled up in the parade ground. A large gang of Labinot's men swarmed around it, and began to unload sacks of flour and carcasses, which were driven on forklift trucks into the main building. Then three long, thin sacks were pulled off and split open. They seemed to contain coffee beans, but as the shiny brown pellets slid away they revealed tell-tale polythene bags at the centre of the sacks. Carlisle whistled.

'What's down there, Pete?' It was Hardy, with the rest of the team at his shoulder.

'About two million quid. Pure heroin. Hang on, there's something going on here.'

A huge man dressed like a medieval warlord strode out of the main complex. A thick sheepskin waistcoat covered most of his frame. Under this he wore a coarse woollen shirt with the sleeves rolled up, revealing hairy, tree-trunk-thick arms. The men parted and he picked up a bag of heroin and held it up for their inspection. They cheered the man, who could only have been Labinot.

Then Labinot turned to the three men who had delivered the cargo. He went as if to slap one of them on the shoulder but instead grabbed the man's jean jacket. With the other hand he whipped out a knife and slit his throat cleanly. Before they could turn and run, the other two men received the same treatment.

Not content with this act of butchery, Labinot strung up one of the bodies at the end of the parade ground. Then he took up a rifle and used the corpse for a spot of shooting practice. His men seemed delighted, if their cheers were anything to go by.

Carlisle didn't bother to relay the details.

'Lousy shot,' was his only comment.

His mind was furiously turning over the possibilities. He concluded that this consignment of heroin must be the last. Labinot wouldn't destroy his own supply base. So if he didn't need any more heroin then he must be planning a big move. The question was, where and into what?

The sun had gone down now and the mercenaries made themselves as comfortable as they could on the hard mountainside. They were woken in the middle of the night by a truck. This one rumbled in from the north. It parked close to the other, abandoned truck and two hard-looking men got out and walked across its headlights. Labinot emerged once again and signalled for something to be brought out. Three polythene sacks were laid out for inspection. Two more men came out of the truck cab and they all inspected the deadly white powder. An agreement seemed to be made and the new truck was opened up for its own cargo to be examined. It was shadowy and difficult to see but something was being exchanged as far as Carlisle could tell.

'They're doing some sort of deal down there,' Carlisle told his eager listeners. 'What the hell have this lot got to swap that's worth two million quid?'

Moley asked a question that cracked the problem: 'How many wheels on the second truck, boss?'

'A lot,' Carlisle said casually, and then as he looked harder his voice rose, suddenly.

'Christ! one hell of a lot. What in Christ's name is in there?'

'Whatever it is it's fucking heavy, right?' asked Moley.

'Check,' answered Carlisle. And then the penny dropped. 'I've got a hunch Mr Labinot's got himself one giant load of weapons-grade plutonium in there.'

'Check,' answered Moley.

Carlisle's response was immediate. He knew there was no time to waste.

'OK, lads, speed of light. Let's get out of here. We're heading south, where we can a start a war between this pair, with a spot of luck.'

Tom had taken the binoculars and the team were almost ready to slip away when the groups of men reassembled below.

'What can you see, Tom?' asked Carlisle.

'Far as I can work out there's some betting going on.'

The drivers from the second truck threw a bag of pure heroin on the ground. The biggest of them stripped to the waist and waited while Labinot's men made their move. A man stepped forward every bit as big as Tomarzo's lover Agron. The excitement grew as the two Goliaths eyed each other and the stakes were finalized.

'Give me the binoculars, Tom.'

Carlisle focused on the tense scene unfolding below. The two men sparred and feinted with each other, then Labinot's man lunged with a savage right hand. He smashed into the other man's face and a long gash opened over his eye. The blood poured from the wound and spread down the man's chest. Blows rained down on him. Then he let go a desperate punch. It made a crunching noise that Carlisle could almost hear from where he was. The jaw of Labinot's man was smashed more than just broken. It hung down on one side and the blood was gushing out, splashing on to the sand until it looked like a red carpet.

As the men fought, the heat and emotional intensity increased around them. Labinot's soldiers clearly had a lot at stake. The screams of encouragement drowned out the noise of two forklift trucks that appeared from the main complex. Both ferried the colossal concrete containers back to a sort of low hangar. They almost tipped over with the weight of their load as they took the steep ramp that probably led under the main fort.

Both fighters were nearing exhaustion now. They looked like fugitives from an abattoir. Hideously gashed and injured, they threw their last, desperate punches at one another. Labinot's man got lucky. He swung a wild punch at the other man and hit his throat. The man fell back, clutching at his windpipe as his opponent moved in for the kill. A second blow hit him to the ground, where he was straddled as punch after sickening punch mashed his face. First a crimson halo seemed to spread around his head and then it turned to a bloom. His face beaten literally to a pulp, the man died right there on the sand.

As Labinot's men howled and whooped at what they saw as their victory, Carlisle's men started to move off. He was about to drop the binoculars when he noticed the other drivers jump into their cab, leaving their dead companion in the dirt. He couldn't believe what he was seeing. As the driver reversed the truck it rolled over the man and then as it moved forward it crushed his body again.

'What sort of bastards are we dealing with here?' Carlisle muttered to himself. Within a few seconds he and his team had disappeared into the darkness.

They had grown more used to the heavy loads and trekked south-west toward Khodja's fortress.

'If these murdering fuckers get a hold here then the region's going to explode,' Carlisle said to Elsa, who was walking beside him. 'What do you think?'

'Eh?'

'I didn't think you'd been listening. What's up?'

'Soon I'm going to be killing my countrymen. I'm not happy with that.'

'Then shape up. I wouldn't care what nationality Khodja and his buddies were. After what I saw them do I'd butcher them like animals. In fact death would be too good for a man like Khodja.'

Carlisle's mind was scanning yet again the horrific image of his friend Mike Greenwood. He knew that it would haunt him until he took revenge. Elsa knew nothing of this and was still troubled.

'But the traditions of this area are warlike. From way . . .' she began.

'Elsa, I have something of an interest in war, as you may have gathered. What Rich and I saw outside that fortress had nothing to do with war. For God's sake, they were just peasants.'

Elsa's eyes opened wide in the moonlight.

'What do you mean, peasants?'

Carlisle wasn't willing to say. As they marched along the gullies and ravines he tried to fend off her insistent questions. Although he stepped up the pace in order to tire her, she came back again and again.

'All right! You want to know,' he exploded at last. 'Now listen to what your noble countrymen are capable of and tell me you won't pull the trigger on them. We woke one morning on our recce and found two prisoners being beaten and tortured by Khodja's men.'

Elsa winced and Carlisle knew he should have stopped then but he went on.

'They thought for a bit more fun they'd castrate them. Yes, they ripped their cocks off and stuffed them in their mouths . . .'

'Stop it! I don't want to hear any more.'

Elsa was so shocked that Carlisle called a halt and rest. She sat away from the rest and was silent for the period of their halt. Carlisle walked over to her before they moved off again.

'Elsa, I have to know that you'll kill if you need to. Whether it's your countrymen or not. I can't risk my men and the mission by carrying a dummy soldier. And that's what you are in your present frame of mind.'

She swung round and the moonlight glinted off her steely eyes. The venom there was so obvious that Carlisle knew that after what she'd just heard she'd kill for fun.

They marched for another hour and a half and Carlisle checked map references with Lane. Eventually he called to the whole team, 'Right, lads, get yourselves round. This is about as far as we go.'

It was barely dawn and they had reached a bend in the mountain road. The rock-face rose sheer to the track and the ground dropped steeply away on the other side.

'This is Khodja's territory. His troop trucks run up and down this stretch. We're going to ambush one of them. If there's men aboard all the better. We waste them but don't damage the truck. That's going on a little holiday up north. So let's get organized.'

Moley and Pug were sent further up the mountain to start a rock fall. The rest were arranged around the area. They'd no sooner found cover than, as luck would have it, they heard the sound of a labouring Mercedes diesel truck. Carlisle grabbed Lane's night sight and confirmed that it was one of Khodja's. By its lack of speed Carlisle judged it must be full.

'Moley, Pug,' he called up to the two strong men.

'PDQ, lads. Get the rocks down on the road. Come on, chop-chop, this one's loaded to the gunwales.'

They had barely got down to level ground when they heard Carlisle's message. The only boulder big enough to cause trouble was an immense rock of some two tons. Moley didn't even pause. He grunted and strained as his squat frame started the thing moving very slightly. Pug, the taller man, piled in and together they shuved and heaved at the boulder as the truck chugged ever nearer. But the rock was obstinate.

'Come on, you bastard,' Pug yelled at his oppo.

'Fuck you, mate. I got it started,' Moley hissed.

Both men's tendons and muscles were straining to breaking point. The truck was now approaching the last bend. They had less than a minute to move the thing.

'Move, you thick bastards, move!' Carlisle called out. But the boulder wouldn't budge and the men were injuring themselves in their attempt.

The truck was still just on the blind side of the bend. Before it came into sight Elsa rose from her cover. She stood in view of Pug and Moley with her shirt half opened. Her beautiful breasts looked coated in honey as they swayed in the mixture of moon and sun light. She looked up imploringly at both men. This and her raw physical presence fired them. In a last titanic effort they rocked the boulder and on the count of two screamed in pain as they forced it down the mountainside.

It thundered down the near-vertical rock-face and

smashed into the mountain track. Then it rocked and almost turned again and rolled over the precipice, where it would have crushed Carlisle, Elsa and Lane. But, as though dragged back, it teetered and settled, blocking the track.

The truck driver braked violently the moment he saw the gigantic boulder. The silence was oppressive. Then the men in the rear of the truck started laughing and chattering. They jumped down and lit cigarettes and waited for the driver to solve the problem.

Carlisle waited for the soldiers to mix and relax, as one or two looked a little trigger-happy. Once the group had settled down he gave the signal. His timing was good. Most of the men had laid their rifles down; those who hadn't were taken out first. The rest panicked and scrabbled around like mice. Carlisle's men emptied their mags in under three seconds and only three men were left alive.

Two scrambled in desperation up the steep mountainside. They thought they were nearing freedom when Pug and Moley opened up on them and blew their heads off their shoulders. The last man threaded through the mayhem and was running like a hare down the mountain track. Elsa watched as he darted off. She let him get a fair way and then lifted her Kalashnikov. Her chin and cheek slid against the butt. She nuzzled the side of her face into the rifle and covered the soldier in her sights. He'd almost escaped when she squeezed the trigger. One shot dropped him. The other mercenaries dragged the bodies to the truck and loaded them on to the back; they would be scattered on Labinot's territory when the time was right. They stripped some of their uniforms and hastily donned them.

Dressed in the dark khaki gear of Khodja's private army, the team first cleared the boulder from the track, then trundled their way to the ammo dump they had uncovered deep in Labinot's territory.

Moley was at the wheel.

'How many did we waste back there?' he asked Carlisle.

'About thirty.'

'They'll be missed then.'

'Not until it's too late. These boys' – his head nodded to the back of the truck – 'are going to start up a little ice-cream war in a few hours.'

'You mean we're gonna slap that Labinot around a bit?'

'Not us, Moley. But Khodja's men are, though. These are their uniforms, aren't they?'

'Too right,' said Moley as he tried to wipe away the blood that was smeared right across his chest.

They reached the ammo dump by mid-morning, loaded up the truck, then rested. Over a brew rustled up by Hardy they listened to Carlisle's plan.

'Around nightfall we'll move out of here as long as the coast is clear. We make a dash for Labinot's bungalow and dig in the observation positions we held yesterday. Now that means the truck will have to be left maybe a mile from the fort. Bear that in mind, because once we've hit Labinot we're going to have to get back to the truck at just over the speed of light. Got me?'

'How hard are we gonna spank him, Pete?' Moley asked.

'Mortars, heat-seeker and our trusty Ks. I think that should give him something to think about.'

'We all head back to the truck?'

'No. Lenny, Pug?' Both men bristled at the sound of their names. 'You two hang low and before the dust settles you get into the fort with all the HE you can carry. I'm certain Labinot will swallow the bait. He's tooled up for a scrap already. With him gone that'll leave a skeleton crew in the fort. Don't touch the hangar, not unless you want to start World War III, but blow the rest to kingdom come. Then leg it down here to the dump and wait for us to get back from Khodja's fireworks party. Don't stay more than two days. If we're not back by then head east to Ohrid. OK?'

Gray just nodded grimly.

'You don't look happy.'

'Well, I just wondered what happens if Labinot *doesn't* take the bait.'

'In that case you and Pug get put against the wall and shot, I would think. That's if they don't torture you to death.'

'I knew I should have stayed in Norwich.'

A little later Elsa slipped away and Carlisle rose a few moments after her.

'I'm just going to freshen up at the spring,' he said as he left.

Gray slipped his beret down to shade his eyes.

'Don't know where he gets the energy from,' he said.

The lads all laughed and before long drifted into sleep.

15

At 2200 hours the diesel was loaded fully and moved off sluggishly. There was light banter but most of the time the men were concentrated and silent, each rehearsing his part in the drama to come. Pug and Gray were in the rear of the truck. The rest squashed into the cab, where their faces were lit by the ghostly light of the dashboard. Just on midnight, beneath a half moon, the truck pulled off the track and stopped. Moley primed the land-mines and quickly got to work. He buried sixteen in all on the 'safe side' of their truck. They were laid in a classic zigzag pattern, allowing no way round the vehicle for any pursuing force. When he got back Carlisle called him over.

'Good work, Moley. That'll give us the head start we need,' he said warmly.

Then he turned to the group as a whole. 'OK, lads, this is it. One hit with the morts and then we spray them with all we've got. Keep your heads down, stay alive and don't do anything silly. We meet back here on completion. Good hunting.' He shook each man by the hand and they moved off.

Ten minutes later they were dug in and had Labinot's fort in their sights. Each had carried one of the blood-spattered corpses from the rear of the truck. They dropped their grisly burdens on the hillside as evidence of an attack by Khodja. Down below the sounds of drunken revelry could be clearly heard.

'Looks like we're in luck, boys. That bet they won has paid for the mother of all beanos by the sound of it. Pug, Lenny, get yourselves down the slope. Pick your own time to move in. Good luck.'

Carlisle and Hardy waited for the OK signal from the two men and trained the mortar. The main complex was surrounded by a chain of low buildings. Some were clearly for storage but most were sleeping quarters. Through the bare windows figures could be seen staggering and lurching in a drunken stupor. Carlisle handed the night sight to Hardy, who was aiming the mortar. 'Get a general look, Rich. We're TG on the sleeping quarters and main complex for afters.'

Hardy scanned the fort and spotted a heavily reinforced shed away from the other buildings.

'There's what can only be an ammo shed over on the left, Pete. Is that TG?'

'Not a bit. We want these bastards armed to the teeth when they head south.'

'Check. Mortar's primed, ready for go.'

'Then let's do it!'

The first shell, the marker, landed fifteen yards from the main complex. It took out the windows in the surrounding low huts. The second shell hit one of the huts dead centre. Bodies and broken glass flew out of the building. The screams and shouts were soon drowned by the blaze that took hold of the structure. In the light from the fire the silhouettes of hundreds of soldiers looked like so many little black mice.

'Open up, lads!' Carlisle roared.

On his command the six Kalashnikovs let their mags loose on full automatic. The mice dropped in dozens. The third mortar hit the main complex and then a forth followed almost immediately. So far there had been no reply. Everyone but Hardy and Carlisle had reloaded and were picking off individual targets when the ominous drone of a helicopter came into earshot.

'Moley, the heat-seeker. Get her ready,' Carlisle bellowed.

Moley dropped his Kalashnikov and positioned the heat-seeking launcher. He'd primed it by the time the helicopter was ranging in on them.

'Go, Moley!' Carlisle yelled as the helicopter opened up on them with a burst of heavy machine-gun fire. The earth and rocks around them were pulverized. Earth and stones fountained all around them. By a miracle no one was hit directly, though a rock splinter had smashed Gray's cheek. He tore open a field-dressing and slapped it on the ugly wound. Seconds later his Kalashnikov was spitting death at the terrified men below. His face and Pug's were flushed with the excitement of battle. Both soldiers were, by any standards, brave men, but in the thick of the fight they became fearless. Pug stood proud against the mountainside. He had a rifle in either hand and as he loosed both weapons he roared a challenge at the fort below to lay waste his magnificent frame if they could.

Hardy laughed at the mad antics of his comrade. Shouting insults of his own at the enemy below, he continued to mortar the fort with deadly effect. The perimeter wall had been breached in two places and the main complex was now ablaze.

The fort was in total chaos. Drunken soldiers were running out of their quarters, many struggling to put their trousers on. It was meat and wine to the deadly marksmen on the mountain. One man had just tied his boots and was reaching for his rifle when Pug yelled to Gray, 'That one, Lenny, before he gets a shot in.'

Both men scored direct hits. The hapless soldier was blown nearly in two.

'Oh well, he died with his boots on,' Pug said wryly.

'Get the feeling he'd like to have kept his head on as well. Still can't have everything,' Gray put in. Then they continued with their deadly purpose.

As the siren wailed out over the besieged fort a semblance of order was emerging. Labinot had appeared. He was easy to spot in his sheepskin waistcoat. He roared orders at his panicking men and slowly they took up positions and started to return fire.

'Don't touch the big man. We need him to lead this

lot against Khodja.' As he said this, Carlisle noticed an armoured personnel carrier revving, preparing to make a dash for the main gate. Its twin machine-gun turret meant it would be more than a match for them if it got out. He yelled to his men, 'TG armoured vehicle heading for main gate. Give it all you've got, lads.' And they did.

Every rifle was trained on the APC but its protection was good. A hundred rounds smashed into it. So many sparks and red-hot splinters were flying off it that it looked like a fireworks display on wheels as it trundled towards the gate. Hardy positioned the mortar and let a shell go. He was way off target. The second shell landed ten yards off and rocked the vehicle, but still it rolled on towards the gate.

'Make this one count, Rich, or we're in deep shit,' hissed Carlisle. The third shell was let fly as the carrier reached the gate and waited for it to open. It landed just beyond the perimeter wall and a mighty explosion followed. A roar went up from Carlisle's team. The gate remained closed.

Meanwhile the helicopter had wheeled round and was coming in for the kill. Moley raised the launcher and for what seemed like an age nothing happened.

'Shoot, you thick bastard!' roared Carlisle.

'It's jammed, Pete. The fucker's jammed.'

Without a second thought Carlisle leapt across and grabbed Moley's Kalashnikov.

'Tom, chuck me the night sight,' he shouted. Lane did so and Carlisle snapped it on his rifle and aimed up at the deadly machine. The pilot was encased in the thickest bulletproofing Carlisle had ever seen. Only a head shot would take him out.

The pilot knew his job. Even as he closed on them he bobbed and weaved his machine, making it an almost impossible target for Carlisle, whose first shot missed by a whisker. He steadied and aimed again, and this time he hit the machine-gunner. With his machine-gun out of commission, the pilot fired his first rocket. The explosion threw Moley and Carlisle high in the air. Both mens were hurled violently some distance from the hit. Carlisle landed heavily, and the crunch of his body hitting the mountainside convinced Elsa he was dead. She dropped her rifle and rushed screaming to his side. She cupped Carlisle's head and pleaded with him to live. His eyes opened and he stared vacantly into her beautiful eyes. His finger pointed up into the air and then to his own head. His eyes closed and he fell into a bottomless pit of darkness.

Elsa had read his message in one. She picked up his rifle and waited for the helicopter to wheel around again. She stood fearlessly against the man and machine who had felled her lover. Pug and Gray pleaded with her to shoot but she would not waver.

'Shoot, for Christ's sake. Shoot,' Lane screamed.

She waited and waited and then, with one deadly shot, turned the pilot's brain to jelly inside his helmet. The helicopter banked violently and went into a spin, finally crashing inside the fort walls. In the light of the explosion Hardy could see armoured trucks beginning to move out. He angled the mortar and took out the nearest one with a single shot. His comrades emptied their magazines into the ranks of Labinot's soldiers, who were now returning fire. Hardy called to the others, 'Time to scoot, lads. We've done enough damage.'

They moved out with bullets zipping all around them. After waving good luck to Pug and Gray, they struggled away with Carlisle on Lane's shoulders and Moley across Hardy's. Elsa carried their weapons as they staggered back to the truck.

Carlisle and Moley were thrown senseless into the rear of the truck. Elsa joined them, and Lane and Hardy leapt into the cab. Hardy took the wheel and they roared into the night.

Labinot's men had opened the main gate and soon APCs and soldiers were pouring out in pursuit. It had covered three hundred yards when the first APC hit the mines. The explosive ripped up through the floor of the vehicle. Those who hadn't died from the blast perished as it plunged off the track and down the steep mountainside. The second carrier hit the last of the mines and exploded as it smashed into the rock-face on its left. This halted the others behind and so allowed Carlisle's team to escape with their battered cargo.

They hurtled down the rough mountain track at breakneck speed. On board were two badly injured men and three deadly fighting units. Left behind were around two hundred dead and injured. A heavy armoured vehicle and helicopter had been taken out, extensive damage inflicted on the fort and two troop trucks destroyed.

And finally two of their mates were still in enemy territory to carry out a perilous mission. Things were hotting up.

16

Lane turned to Hardy and asked, 'Just as a matter of interest, where are we heading?'

'Just as a matter of interest, I'm fucked if I know. The hell out of here'll do for the moment. After that, ask the boss.'

'I don't think he's in too good a shape to answer at the moment,' said Lane gloomily.

'How bad are they?'

'Well, that was a pretty bad knock they both took. Still, nurse Elsa's doing the business in the back there. We'll have to wait and see,' said Lane, shrugging.

'I wouldn't mind a bang on the head if it meant her giving me a bit of treatment.'

'Know what you mean. The boss is smitten, by the look of it. You've served under him before. Does he go for the fillies as a rule?'

'You must be joking. I've never seen him even sniff before.'

That was what Lane had suspected.

'Funny, 'cos I'd swear he'd use her shit for tooth-paste if you gave him half a chance.'

'Just give *me* half a chance,' laughed Hardy.

The two men drove along the mountain road bantering in this vein. In truth it was to mask their unease about the condition of both their comrades, but especially Carlisle. Both men realized that he could take very little more. And both hoped that at any moment Elsa would tap on the cab window and give the all-clear.

Instead she banged loudly and her face said the opposite was the case.

Lane could read the alarm signals loud and clear. He scrambled from the offside window and climbed to the rear of the truck. Elsa was becoming frantic.

'His temperature is critical, Tom. He's going to die. You've got to stop. You've got to.' She thumped on his chest in frustration and anger. Lane tried to calm her but he could see the cause was lost. Instead he leant over to where both injured men lay. Moley was in pretty bad shape too. He'd vomited twice and his temperature was dangerously high, but he would probably live, Lane reckoned.

One look at Carlisle said he probably wouldn't. His brow was like a furnace. Yet there was a cold clamminess about him that Lane had seen all too often before. It was the cold sweat that foreshadowed pneumonia and death.

'We'll stop over at the ammo dump,' he said. He didn't quite know what they could do there but if they carried on in the truck on that rough road, Carlisle wouldn't see the daylight. Lane drummed on the cab window and mouthed the message. Hardy nodded and checked the map for the turn-off.

The decision saved their lives. No sooner had they found the turning and hidden the truck among the pines than another of Labinot's helicopters swept over them.

'Where the fuck did that come from?' said Hardy.

'Search me, they must have a radio link with someone. We knocked out the only one they had.'

'So if that bloke Labinot can rustle up a full-combat helicopter what else has he got up his sleeve?' As he spoke, Hardy's mind was with Pug and Gray. They would be expecting a soft target. It might just be that things were getting hot back at the fort. Lane could read the concern on his face.

'Problem, Rich?'

'Pug and Lenny.'

'I was thinking the same.'

The two men stared at each other, knowing that a crisis was on the way. Both realized for a moment what it was like to be in Carlisle's shoes.

'Let's see what we can do for the boss,' said Hardy.

Elsa had covered both Moley and Carlisle with blankets from the dump. She'd brought cold water from the spring and was dabbing their foreheads. Moley was turning around and moaning in his sleep. Carlisle was burning. His pulse was fading, and his breathing was deep and ominously rhythmic – the way people breathe on life-support machines. But

Carlisle had no machine helping him. Hardy took a thermometer from an ancient medical kit he'd found. It showed 108°F.

'Fuck me, he should be dead.'

Elsa stared down at the man she loved. Her tears were splashing on to his burning face. Lane and Hardy, if they could have, would have cried as well.

'There's a root – it grows at a much lower altitude. It might help,' she said, a look of hope flickering across her face.

'How much lower?'

'Three hundred metres at the most.'

A thousand feet. That would mean crossing the winding mountain road a dozen times. Hardy knew what she had in mind. But it was far too risky. He turned to her and said as tenderly as he could, 'It's dangerous out there, Elsa. Labinot's men are pouring down. We'll be shot on sight.'

Elsa said nothing but gazed into his eyes with such a longing that there was nothing more to discuss.

'I'll go, Tom,' he said. 'No point in us both getting killed. Elsa, ready?'

'Ready,' she answered. In moments they were gone.

Lane stayed by his two injured comrades. Moley was coming to. The strong man's will to survive was dragging him back to life. Lane scampered over to the dump and got the stove going. The first thing Moley saw when he opened his eyes was a steaming mug of tea.

'Thanks, Mum,' he said with a grimace as Lane handed him the brew.

The two of them waited in the fading moonlight. Another helicopter flew over them and the steady rumble of trucks and armoured vehicles said Labinot was on the move. They heard a sudden rattle of a machine-gun. Both men tensed, fearing the worst. The time slid by as the night sky above them turned in its usual giant cartwheel. The faintest glow of morning sun was spreading in the east. Lane looked at Carlisle's tortured face. The leader's breathing was becoming erratic.

Moley and Lane looked each other in the eye. Elsa and Hardy had been gone nearly two hours. Time was running out.

'We can't give them much longer, Tom,' said Moley, propping himself up.

'We can't just leave them either,' replied Lane, knowing all the while that that was what they might have to do.

'I vote we take Pete and the truck north and pick up Lenny and Pug,' said Moley.

'And then what?'

'Scram. We've done the best we could.'

'But Rich risked his life for you. We can't just run out and . . .'

Moley's iron-hard features were set in a grim and determined mask. There was no malice or fear or betrayal. He had simply spoken the truth and Lane knew it.

'Face facts, Tom. Rich is fit and strong. It wouldn't take him more than a couple of hours to get down a thousand feet of mountain. Those shots we heard – I reckon that was them, mate.'

Lane set about gathering essential equipment for the dash north. When Moley walked over unsteadily to console him he shrugged and nodded his head wearily.

'You're right, Moley. They're not coming back.'

'Who's not?' It was Hardy. He had burst from a pine thicket with Elsa behind him.

'What the hell!'

Lane and Moley were so glad to see their return they didn't know whether to kiss Elsa or Hardy.

Elsa set about grinding the root they'd collected and Hardy lit the stove to boil up the water. He spoke as he worked.

'We were very nearly fucked, believe me. Labinot's got World War III, on the road out there. One of the 'copters spotted us and took a pot-shot or two. We had to circle round a mile or more but they're off our tails now. Anyway, they're desperate to get at Khodja, by the look of things.'

'Richard, quickly the water,' said Elsa. Then she took the saucepan, crushed the root in the water and rushed to Carlisle. She spooned minute drops between his lips and gently rested his head on a folded combat jacket.

'How long before it works?' asked Hardy.

'I don't know,' Elsa answered.

With no other choice, the four of them sat by Carlisle and waited. Up in the sky there were eagles circling in the rising thermals. Elsa lay her head next to Carlisle and watched the patterns the birds made. She was looking for some magical sign that would say he would live.

Exhaustion dragged her and the others into a deep but troubled sleep. The first one to wake was Carlisle. He blinked in the bright daylight and turned to Elsa. Her eyes opened and filled with tears as she began to sob with relief.

17

As soon as they heard the Mercedes truck pull away, Pug and Gray buried the HE. Then they began to dig hidey-holes in the sandy soil further down the mountain, away from the old positions, for they knew that Labinot's men would be swarming over the area. Within ten minutes or so the two men were concealed in shallow pits with only a narrow breathing hole to betray their whereabouts. They waited.

Soon the roar of the pursuing trucks being blown to pieces by the mines drifted to the men in their hides. Then the wild chatter of the soldiers sounded in their ears as Labinot's men found the corpses planted by the mercenaries.

Not content with the men's deaths, they hacked their heads off and mutilated their bodies as they screamed at them in frenetic Albanian.

'We must have stuffed this lot pretty badly,' whispered Gray.

'I reckon an hour and they'll be on the warpath. Let's sleep while we can.'

The two men pushed their mouths to the breathing

hole and slept as best they could. When they woke it was still dark. The rumble of trucks and other vehicles seemed endless but eventually silence returned and they knew the fort was theirs for the taking.

'Lenny?'

'I hear you, Pug. What's the plan?'

'We want to get in while it's still dark. I reckon that means we've got about an hour. There's the breach about thirty yards off. I reckon there'll be a guard or two. Take them out and bingo.'

'Sounds OK to me. Let's just get out of these rat holes, can we? I'm choking to death in here.'

As Gray spoke a snake slithered into the space he was vacating. Every molecule in his body started to supercharge. The world seemed to be in slow motion as he raised his knife and came down on it. The snake had no chance. Gray's knife had sliced it twice before it could even move. But the violence of his attack had raised the alarm with the guards by the breached perimeter wall. In fact they thought it was the remains of Khodja's men in their death throes. Joking callously, the three men ambled to where the noise seemed to have come. When they got there they didn't find scattered helpless casualties. They found Pug in full flow. They didn't last a second. Three Albanian bodies now lay with the snake in the shallow pit on the mountainside.

Pug and Lenny stole into the fort and took cover. Once the coast seemed clear they made their move. The fort was eerily silent, and the stench of burning bodies hung in the air. The two men headed for the main complex. They skirted round and found an air vent. Pug levered the cover off and they crawled inside.

The vent was narrow enough without the encumbrance of the high explosive. But inch by inch they moved forward until Gray reached a heavy metal grille.

'Come on, you fat bastard,' Gray called to Pug.

'Listen, weasel, there's times when old Pug's muscle comes in handy. Don't knock it.'

'I don't, Pug. I just don't want to spend Christmas in here.'

The room beyond the grille was in darkness. It was impossible to know what was beyond. It smelt musty like a museum.

'Pass me the pencil torch, Pug. I'll check this room out,' said Gray.

Pug had to wriggle and contort to get the torch out in the confined space. He was sweating profusely as he handed it to Gray.

'I hope there's something worth looking at after all this palaver.'

Gray shone the torch into the darkened room. For maybe a full minute he said nothing. A full minute in that cramped space was a long time, and Pug nudged him and said, 'Come on, Lenny, what's in there that's so interesting?'

'Jesus Christ, Pug! You wouldn't believe me if I told you, mate.'

'Try me,' snapped Pug, who was getting irritable in the hot, confined space.

Gray still didn't answer him but pushed the grille firmly aside and slid into the mysterious room. Pug followed as fast as he could and fell into a crumpled heap on the floor. When he got up his mouth gaped, just like his pal's.

'Fuck me, what the hell's this?'

In front of the astonished men was a scene like a cross between something out of Indiana Jones and a Dennis Wheatley novel.

The room was about thirty feet square. At one end was an altar. At its head, instead of a cross, was a stuffed goat's head. At either end there were candlesticks with black candles and behind everything the Nazi flag – a black swastika on a white circle with a red background.

All around the walls were black and white photographs of Hitler. In most he was parading or being driven past adoring crowds or troops. There were a few, however, that the world had never seen. These showed him standing in front of the disguised fort that Khodja now occupied.

'What the hell is that?' asked Pug, who'd not yet seen the fortress.

'Search me, but the country looks like Albania,' said Gray, then he turned to look at the rest of the room. It was crammed with Nazi memorabilia: death's-head daggers, leather gauntlets, caps with SS badges, and uniforms formerly worn by officers of the highest rank.

'Fuck me, what the hell's this?' said Pug.

'You gonna learn another tune?' Gray protested.

'I just can't take it in, mate. All this stuff's been here since the last war.'

'Looks like it. There's dealers back home who'd give their right arm to get hold of this lot. But what I can't work out is ...' He tailed off as the torch played on one of the photographs. His eyes widened as he walked over for a closer inspection, and they were nearly popping out of his head when he turned to Pug.

'Christ! Look, go on. Just look and tell me who that is?'

He pointed to a Nazi officer standing next to Hitler. The lean, almost gaunt, features, along with a haughtiness, looked very familiar.

'I know that face but I can't place it,' said Pug.

'OK then, try that one for size.'

Gray pointed at the photo next to it. The same figure was standing in front of a row of corpses. They had all been shot, by the look of it. The town in the background was without any doubt Salonika.

'Fuck me, that's ... no, the hair's wrong. That bloke's got blond hair. But otherwise it's Tomarzo.'

'That, Pug, is our mate Tomarzo's dad. Shit! It all fits together now. That's what all the interest is. Tomarzo wants this lot back and probably more.'

They was about to look more closely at the other photographs lining the walls when they heard a noise outside.

'Quick, the vent,' hissed Gray.

'No time. Get behind the table.'

In a flash they had replaced the grille and dived under the altar table. The door swung open and six large men walked in. The last to enter was Labinot. He was easy to recognize in his shepherd's waistcoat. From where they were the two mercenaries could smell the rich food and alcohol on him. Half his meal was down his front.

All the men assembled in front of the altar, and Labinot addressed the goat's head with his arms spread wide. He bowed at the end of his speech and then walked to a table and took one of the three death's-head daggers. His voice was getting louder as he seemed to implore first the large photo of Hitler, then the altar, and finally his men. After each outburst he drew the dagger across his forearm. The wounds were pouring with blood, which was caught in a goblet. Each man drank in turn the blood of his leader.

Then, as they stood solemnly in front of the altar, a sheep was bought in. The animal was held high in the air and presented to the goat's head. It was then laid gently on the table above Gray's and Pug's heads. Through a minute tear in the cloth Gray saw something he would never forget.

Labinot raised the knife. In a single sweep he opened up the animal. Then he tore out the heart and ate it. It was still pumping as his teeth ripped it apart. The men roared their approval and the whole party left as one.

'Jesus, what the fuck was all that about, Pug?' whispered Gray.

'Some ritual to give them victory over the geezer in the south, I suppose.'

'What, Khodja? Christ, I wouldn't want to be in his shoes when they get there. They're fucking maniacs,' said Gray.

'And there's our lads as well, remember.'

'Pete and the boys'll be ready for them. Labinot won't have a chance.'

They laughed at this little exaggeration but both feared for their comrades facing such a ruthless enemy.

It was clear to them as they made their way around the main complex that almost all of Labinot's men had gone south. If they worked fast they could blow the fort to pieces and escape in the same direction, maybe joining the others for the big battle.

The walls were thick and the charges would have to be carefully chosen. They worked their way down the darkened corridors to get a feel of the place.

As long as they moved silently, it was easy to avoid running into Labinot's men. The corridors of the fort were big and full of echoes, and twice they heard men coming and were able to find a doorway to dive into. When they had recced the whole place they agreed the main charges should be placed at the centre of the structure. The fort was built around a sort of central tower which, when it collapsed, would pull down everything with it. In the very centre of the fort was a main hall.

Apparently medieval in construction, it was heavy and overbearing. Gray eyed it with awe.

'Christ, when this lot blows there'll be no chance for anyone left in there,' he said.

'Let them worry about that,' growled Pug. 'Come on, this place gives me the creeps. Sooner we're out of here the better.'

They turned to head back to the room where they'd left the HE. Staggering a few feet from them was one of the men who'd been present at the sacrifice. Very drunk, he called loudly to them in Albanian.

'*Shejpko*!'

Neither man responded to what must have been a command because he bellowed the word at them again. Pug walked forward and was close enough for the man, even in his present state, to recognize one of Khodja's uniforms. Before he had a chance to say another word Pug nailed him. His head crashed into the hard stone wall behind him and he was dead before he hit the ground.

'That's it, mate, now let's go. I reckon he'll be missed in an hour or so,' said Pug, rubbing his knuckles. 'Come on, we'll get him back to that room and stick him in the vent.'

They did this in double-quick time. Then, when the coast looked clear, they moved about the fort like two shadows.

Within an hour they'd planted over two hundred-weight of high explosive. The sounds of Labinot's men were never far away, though, and when they'd primed the last charge and plumbed it to the radio detonator, they felt a wave of relief. Their Browning automatics would have been no match for the Albanians had there been any real trouble. But as usual, stealth and timing had won the day.

'What's the range on the radio detonator, Lenny?'

'About four hundred yards. We can let them all go from the position on the mountain.'

'Yeah, but only after Labinot's gone to the races. Remember, the boss wants him down there to give that Khodja some gyp.'

'That won't be long, judging by the war dance they were all getting up to an hour ago. Let's get back to the vent and get out of here.'

'Check,' called Pug and strapped the radio detonator to his inner leg as they made their way out. The air-vent grille seemed to have jammed. Gray was wrestling with it as Pug took a last look at the room. Gray finally tore the grille away and called out in alarm.

'Pug, the body's gone.'

It was the last thing he remembered of the room as a heavy blow came down on the back of his skull. Seconds later a rifle butt smashed into Pug's head and the big man dropped. He grabbed out as he went down and pulled the altar cloth and the grinning goat's head to the ground.

18

Carlisle's head felt like an elephant had trodden on it. The sun hurt his eyes and the chatter of the lads round the stove was like a firecracker going off in his brain. But he was alive. Just.

Elsa brought him tea and food from the compo rations.

'You can't carry on this way, Peter. The root I found for you is the most powerful I know. You had three times the amount an injured person should need.'

'Only three,' joked Carlisle. 'That could only have been a graze I took then.'

Elsa knew as he spoke so casually about his terrible wounds that morning that nothing would change this man. Destiny had flung them together but his fate remained his own. She looked down into the soft, slate-blue eyes of the only man she had ever loved. For him it was honour and the unceasing fight for freedom. For her it must be Albania. That was how it was.

Carlisle called the lads over and after checking on

Moley's health – he was almost back to normal – he outlined the plan.

'We travel light again, lads, and at night. It's worked so far, so no reason to change things now. Once we get to within a mile of Khodja's fort we dig in and wait for the action to begin. Most important is the destruction of the fortress. Get that done and whatever forces they have left will have to be kept on the hoof. Then they'll be ripe for picking off.'

The men cleared the site meticulously. Only the closest of inspections would reveal that anyone had been there at all. In the evening the truck was camouflaged.

The carry weapons were essential. Carlisle also insisted on an anti-tank launcher. Weighing nearly two hundred pounds, it was loaded on to Moley's broad shoulders. He balanced the weight and the shells were added. He had over sixteen stone on his back.

'Wagons roll,' Carlisle called out, grinning, and the torturous trek to Khodja's fortress began.

By morning they were dug into a high ridge that looked down from a thousand feet over the main track from the north. Well camouflaged, they had clear views around the compass. To their left and down the mountainside were the white domes of Khodja's stronghold, silent and menacing. Carlisle took up the binoculars and trained them on the area in front of the fort – the place where the two peasants had been butchered. He knew his friend had died there too.

Mike's mutilated body had hung from the very tree he had in focus. One chance, that was all he wanted. Lane nudged Carlisle.

'Pete, there's some movement on the opposite ridge.'

A platoon of Labinot's men had gained some high ground above the fort and were digging mortar positions.

'Good, that's what I like to see. Sound textbook soldiering. Now let the fuckers beat the shit out of each other.'

This was what they clearly intended to do. The drone of the helicopters and the armoured-vehicle back-up both signalled that the battle was close. The first mortars were woefully off target but then they found their mark. The largest of the domes took a direct hit and blew apart. Labinot's helicopters swooped down like the eagles of their country. They fired rockets at the shattered dome and the first flames darted into the air.

'There's a trap here. Khodja's men haven't even fired a round yet. They want to gauge Labinot's strength and then zap him,' said Carlisle.

'If they can; their fortress has taken plenty of damage already,' replied Lane.

'Chicken feed. That thing goes right into the mountain. Labinot might as well be throwing brickbats at him. If he's got any sense Khodja will stay put. Labinot can't get in and he's got nowhere to go but home.'

By now Labinot's armoured vehicles had found the

open ground and were heading for the apparently beleaguered fortress. The helicopters rocketed the main entrance and crippled the doors.

'Interesting. Just what is he going to do now?' mused Carlisle.

Moments later he was to find out. Khodja had dragged all but Labinot's reserve platoons into action. As in a game of chess, the Queen had been making merry, culling pawns here and there.

Now Labinot's positions were hopelessly exposed. The half hour of mayhem, and the burning domes of Khodja's fortress were about to be accounted for.

The first blows were heat-seeking missiles fired at the exposed attacking helicopters. Almost simultaneously they exploded and brought both helicopters crashing to the ground. One came down on a mortar position and the secondary explosion rocked a passing armoured vehicle. It crashed into a troop carrier and as it exploded whole bodies and dismembered parts were flung high over a pine copse, where they hung in the branches like obscene Christmas-tree decorations.

Labinot, who'd joined his troops just that morning, could see the day was being lost. His burly figure strode from cover. In clear line of fire, he signalled to the mortars to cease. Then he withdrew his armoured vehicles.

'Now he's getting smart,' said Carlisle. The whole Napoleonic scene below quite fascinated him. 'Khodja's about to make a big mistake unless all my soldiering instincts have deserted me. Don't think he's read up his classic battles.'

Lane and Hardy stared in fascination as Carlisle's prediction unfolded.

'Which ones, Pete?' asked Lane.

'Try Hastings.'

Then as he saw tell-tale movements around the fortress, Carlisle yelled at his men.

'OK, chaps, we're "go"!'

They picked up their equipment and were battle-ready in seconds.

'We drop five hundred feet to the overhang. This lot are entering their own private Armageddon. In an hour we'll have some mopping up to do.'

As the team tumbled down the mountain the battle below entered a more savage stage.

The fortress, which had looked seamless except for the great reinforced doors, now sprouted moving panels. From the side of the buildings half of Khodja's force poured forth: two tanks, armoured assault vehicles, and platoon after platoon of infantry.

Three helicopters swept up from low ground and pounced on Labinot's retreating ground troops. Finally Khodja, who had emerged from his eyrie by now, directed his mortar positions to pound Labinot with everything.

The mortars were concealed in camouflaged nests and opened up with terrible effect. With his assault vehicles in retreat Labinot's infantry dived for what meagre cover they could find. At least a hundred perished under the combined mortar and helicopter attack.

Hardy had grabbed the binoculars.

'They're goners, Pete. This'll be over in twenty minutes.'

'Don't bank on it, Rich. That bastard Labinot's sent his men like lambs to the slaughter. But he's dragged Khodja out now. Watch this space.'

As he spoke Labinot's mortar teams reappeared again. They hadn't retreated but thrown camouflage nets over themselves. Now, from the high ground, they let loose a murderous barrage on the infantry below. As the defending helicopters moved to attack them the retreating assault vehicles swivelled and charged back. A heavy machine-gun was trained on one of the helicopters. Two bursts brought it down. The volatile fuel tank exploded on impact with the ground and at least three platoons of Khodja's men were engulfed in flames. They squirmed and fried like ants in boiling water. As the battle raged on, the repulsive and unmistakable smell of burning bodies even penetrated Carlisle's position.

Then, with no warning, came the hiss of high-explosive artillery shells, raining down on Khodja's mortar positions. He'd cleverly concealed them two miles to the north. The approximate mortar positions were radioed to the guns and they pounded the concealed areas remorselessly. Gigantic explosions marked a direct hit, and slowly Khodja's attack was failing.

His Czech-built tanks seemed to be his trump card. There were five in all now, and they rumbled across the sandy ground and took out all before them. The psychological advantage had swung once again in Khodja's favour. His remaining helicopter rocketed and machine-gunned the mortar positions and all but annihilated them. It wheeled round to join the advancing tanks and Labinot's men were in panic.

Carlisle had a split-second decision to make. If he let Khodja take the day then he had half an army to contend with. If he opened up on Khodja's pursuing tanks and helicopter then their position was blown and they'd have to take their chances with whatever the outcome was.

The decision was crucial to the success of the mission. Everything hung in the balance now. He should have made a cold-blooded rational choice. Probably it should have been to allow Khodja the day and then pick off his weakened forces. But as the advantage had swung to the southern warlord his confidence had grown. Now, high in the turret of an armoured assault vehicle, he urged his forces on. He waved a Kalashnikov high above his head and pointed it at the retreating Labinot. Above the din his shouts must have been heard because his men responded and roared as they charged forward. The sight of this heathen with his bloodthirsty mob was more than Carlisle could stomach.

'Moley, prime the anti-tank launcher,' he yelled.

Hardy, Lane and Moley worked fast and the only

heavy weapon they'd brought down with them was ready before Khodja's advancing forces had crossed their line.

'Just say it, Pete,' said Moley.

Carlisle had taken hold of Elsa's Kalashnikov. He had Khodja's massive head in his sights. His finger stroked the trigger and then pulled back. Death, he decided, was too easy for this creature.

'How many shells, Tom?'

'Three, boss.'

'Take out the leader and the rear two. That should keep them guessing for a while.'

Moley positioned the launcher and waited. Carlisle had the helicopter pilot in his rifle sights. The two attacks would have to be simultaneous.

'The range is perfect, Pete,' barked Moley.

'Wait.'

'We'll lose them, Pete.'

'Wait now . . . and . . .'

'Pete, the front tank's beyond . . .'

'Shoot!'

The front tank was beyond nothing except self-preservation. Moley's coordinates, once locked, spelt its certain doom. It all but vaporized under the direct hit. At that same moment Carlisle sent the helicopter and its crew to eternity. His Kalashnikov splashed the pilot's brains across the cabin and with his hand still jammed in the controls the helicopter crashed into the mountain.

Moley's second and third shells were as deadly as

the first. They destroyed two more tanks and crippled a third. Now, with only one tank operative and with the battle swung for the second and decisive time against him, Khodja went into full retreat.

Labinot's logical decision would be to regroup and smash Khodja with one decisive blow. But what man, with his bitter enemy in his sights, can act logically? He ordered a full attack and the battle entered its final, most gruesome stage: hand-to-hand combat.

This played straight into Carlisle's hands. With the two armies snuffing each other out and the fort in the north destroyed, his mission was within sight of completion. His men had vanished from their position. It wasn't lost on them that Labinot would be very curious to find his mysterious helpers once the battle was over.

'We'll get up the mountain, lads. If Labinot turns on us then we'll at least have a head start,' he told his team.

But Labinot had other fish to fry. The calamitous noise of heavy weapons had been replaced by the sinister rattle of machine-guns and automatics. Khodja's men were doomed. They couldn't retreat or they would be picked off. They had instead to hold out in isolated pockets and hope to escape under cover of night.

Labinot was wise to this and forced his men to surge on. But they could only inch forward under intense and desperate rearguard fire. As the day wore

on, the screams of wounded men or those about to
die echoed through the mountains.

'They're stubborn bastards, all right,' said Moley.

'Wouldn't you be? If they can hold out till night then
they've at least got a dog's chance,' replied Carlisle.

As he spoke a group of Khodja's men were ferreted
out of their sniper nest. Their luck had run out. They
held their hands high in submission. Before they
had time to lower them again, they were dead. The
man who'd machine-gunned them was Labinot himself. He and his men moved through the tight gullies
and ravines like hunting dogs.

'There's not many left, you know,' Lane told
Carlisle.

'No, as Wellington said at Waterloo, it was a damn
close-run thing. If Khodja could organize something
now he'd have a chance.'

But unknown to Carlisle and his men, Khodja had
escaped. He'd taken a bodyguard and at least a million
pounds' worth of heroin with him. The fortress had
countless chambers and tunnels. Some emerged as far
as a mile from the battlefield. He and his bodyguard
had taken one of these.

By early evening all resistance was over. There were
prisoners who'd been put to one side. Any hope of
their receiving clemency evaporated as Labinot set
about one of his favourite pastimes. He stood atop
the only remaining armoured vehicle as each prisoner
was brought before him to plead his case.

'What do you think they're saying?' asked Hardy

as he and the others watched the cruel scene from afar.

'Something like, "I always admired you, great leader Labinot, let me live and I'll give you my goats, my daughter and my very own arsehole if you so desire,"' said Carlisle.

The men all laughed, but fell silent as the first of the prisoners was handed up to Labinot. His hands were bound and his head snapped back as his throat was cut. Blood spurted over the other thirty or so prisoners. They panicked and Labinot and the rest of his men set about hunting them down. They squealed with laughter as they slit their throats. Carlisle could see that some of the men were removing body parts as trophies.

The battered fortress gaped at them. The great black hole of an entrance was at their mercy. But Labinot was no fool. It had probably been booby-trapped. He aimed the cannon from the armoured vehicle and blasted off a few rounds. The dust settled and he and his men – there were no more than two hundred left now – marched towards their final trophy.

A man rose from the turret of the armoured vehicle and called loudly to his leader. The triumphant party came to a standstill. The man rushed from the truck and spoke directly to Labinot, who, after a pause, walked quickly to the vehicle. He waved his arm and his men rushed back to the troop carriers. Within ten minutes the battered column was heading north. Carlisle and his men let out a huge roar. It must have been the news that the fort had been blown.

'Gentlemen,' announced Carlisle with great solemnity, 'and ladies, of course. I think I can safely say that we have only to pick over the grisly bones of a certain Mr Khodja and mop up the battered remnants of Mr Labinot's army and our mission is close to an end.'

He couldn't have been more wrong.

19

Khodja's dreaded stronghold was smashed. Inside, the labyrinth of tunnels was empty and quiet. Carlisle and his men searched through the rubble. Bodies were dotted around and Hardy bent close to look at the uniform of one. He'd seen something that jogged his memory. The buttons.

'Hey, Pete, the buttons on this coat are the same as the one I picked up after that scrap on Lake Ohrid.'

Carlisle ripped one of the buttons from the coat and looked at it more closely.

'That's an SS button.'

As he said it he was lost in thought. Something didn't quite fit. There was something he couldn't quite figure out. Had they stayed longer and had they opened one more door in the complex of hundreds they would have found a room almost identical to the one Pug and Gray had found in the north. Everything would have become crystal-clear then. Instead Carlisle started the hunt for Khodja.

'Come on, lads, I reckon he's gone south or east. Any ideas?' he asked.

This drew a blank. Who could tell? Then Elsa came forward.

'I can find out. Let me go to my village.'

This was a bombshell to them all, but especially to Carlisle.

'Your village! You never said you came from this area. I assumed . . .'

'You never asked. I'll be back in an hour with Khodja's whereabouts.'

Before there was time to argue Elsa had threaded past the rest and vanished into the dark.

Moley moved closer to Carlisle.

'How do we know we can trust her?'

Carlisle looked only once at him and there were no more questions. They sat in silence in the starlit Albanian night. Suddenly there was a moan. It was someone in pretty bad pain.

'Quick, lads,' said Hardy, and instinctively the rest followed. The sound led them to a soldier trapped between two rocks. He'd been shot and had fallen, probably breaking both legs and at the same time jamming himself in tight. His eyes looked up at the Englishmen imploringly. It was a pathetic sight.

'Have we got a field medic kit?' Hardy asked the group. He intended to give the soldier a morphine shot and let him at least die in peace.

'Yes,' came the answer to his question. It was Carlisle, who then walked out and shot the man through the head. 'That's the only medic kit that bastard's getting.'

Before there was time for any further discussion Elsa burst into the arena.

'He's heading east for the lake.'

'Can we cut him off?'

'If we have a truck then I can find a road.'

'Moley?'

'Should be able to get something going round here, boss.'

As Moley set about providing transport the others wired up Khodja's fort with all the HE they could lay their hands on. Had they only looked for a short while they would have found secrets. Secrets that would have made history tell a very different story. But the secrets of a generation were blown into eternity as Carlisle touched the radio control.

Half the mountain seemed to shake and then silence settled like the dust. Two minutes later they were heading for Lake Ohrid.

'Bet Lenny and Pug have had some fun up there,' said Hardy.

'Hope so,' was all Carlisle would say. His stomach was so tight he was almost vomiting as the truck slithered down the primitive track. He was running through a thousand outcomes to the meeting they were making for. When they arrived there was nothing but the placid lapping water.

They waited by the lake for some while. Any noise would carry an enormous distance in the clear night air. When they heard a sound it was, by chance, amazingly close. A hundred yards away Khodja and

230

what was left of his men scampered noisily on to the shore of the lake.

'Give me the night sight, Tom,' Carlisle whispered.

He slid the night sight on his rifle and scanned the eight men down the shore. They looked burly and arrogant. They were laughing and smoking as they stood waiting. No doubt the joke was to do with the poor bastards left behind. None was more slap-happy than Khodja. Then Carlisle opened up on full auto and only Khodja was left standing.

Carlisle had expected him to run for cover. Instead he looked in the direction of the shots and smiled. He walked towards them with a confident swagger. His bearing seemed to imply that this was no problem.

When he arrived at the circle of five mercenaries he dumped the bag of pure heroin at his feet. The icy look he got said 'no dice'. Khodja seemed to know what was going to happen. He held the palms of his hands wide and shrugged. Then Carlisle stepped forward and hit him with all his might. The giant Albanian fell and lay on the shore. Carlisle kicked him in the groin. The power of the blow smashed Khodja's genitals yet he made no sound. When Carlisle kicked him again he just gurgled slightly. He pulled Khodja's face up close to his own. There was no terror in his eyes as Carlisle had expected; in fact, the opposite. They gleamed with defiance.

'Hold him,' commanded Carlisle.

His men obliged with great reluctance. It was a terrible spectacle: their leader turned into a subhuman before their eyes. Carlisle took his knife and slashed the Albanian's face into a hideous, bloody mess. The man's nose was barely hanging on. Carlisle rubbed his hand in the blood and showed it to Khodja.

'Look, you animal,' he bellowed. 'Look, you did this to my friend. You fucking animal!' He kicked his groin again but Khodja did nothing but stare into his enflamed eyes.

'What does it feel like? Go on, tell me.'

Khodja looked at him with a weird grin on his blood-spattered face. Carlisle wanted him to beg. He needed him to beg. He turned to Elsa.

'Tell him what I'm going to do. Tell him I'm going to cut his eyes out and mutilate him. Tell him! Tell the bastard he's about to be castrated.'

Elsa rattled off a sentence in Albanian. Her voice was cold and mechanical. The man said nothing in reply. Instead the resigned look in his eyes seemed to tell Carlisle to get on with it.

The men had no stomach for any more. Hardy shouted to his friend, 'For God's sake, Pete, finish him. He's taunting you, man. This is his final victory. Do it, Pete!'

Carlisle knew this was true. His head dropped and he closed his eyes. He opened them and took out his revolver. Wearily he raised the weapon and held it to Khodja's forehead.

'Let him go, lads.'

Hardy and Moley stood back. Carlisle glanced at Elsa and told her to translate. She repeated the

blocks of words as Carlisle went on. 'Khodja . . .
in the name of humanity . . . for obscene crimes
carried out against the aforesaid . . . as well as the
unholy destruction of a good and noble friend . . . I
sentence you to death.'

As Elsa finished, the Albanian spat in Carlisle's face.
A single shot between the eyes sent him to whatever
god he prayed to. The body dropped to the ground
and half rolled into the lake, where the water lapped
over what was left of his face. Carlisle turned to leave
and as he did so small groups of terrified fishermen
appeared from behind rocks where they'd hidden.
One walked towards Hardy and with no warning
dived at him and brought him to the ground with a
rugby tackle. In the same instant Carlisle raised his CZ
and shot a hunched figure ten yards away. It was one
of Khodja's bodyguards. He'd been wounded when
Carlisle had opened up on the group earlier. He'd
crawled the hundred yards along the shore, bent on
a final act of vengeance.

The fisherman had seen him raise his gun and had
dived to save Hardy's life. In so doing he'd caught
the bullet through his neck and died instantly. They
rolled him over. It was the man Hardy had spared on
his other fateful visit to the lake.

'Let's get out of here,' said Carlisle.

Hardy took the wheel as they wound their way up
the mountain and reached the main track heading
north. They were all relieved to have the scene on
the lake in the past. It had been painful to see

Carlisle in such torment. And worse to see him reduced to a snarling animal instead of the fine man he was.

'The ammo dump's only about twenty miles. Don't overdo the speed. This old crock won't stand for it,' said Moley.

So it was that they rolled gently through the moonlit valleys with seemingly all the time in the world. They were in for a rude shock.

'Here we are, gentlemen, the OK Hotel,' said Hardy as they reached the ammo dump. 'I hope your bed of pine needles has been booked in advance.'

They rolled out and called for Pug and Gray to stop joking about.

'All right, children, hide-and-seek's over. Come on out and give us all the news,' called Carlisle. The whole crew knew Gray as a great practical joker and all expected him to have prepared some little surprise for them. Only gradually as they dug around did the awful truth sink in.

'They're not here, Pete,' said Hardy.

'I think you're right, Rich.'

Carlisle's mind was back in overdrive. He computed a dozen possibilities before he blurted the probable truth out. 'They're dead or Labinot's got them.'

A shudder went through the group. The very thought of their mates being in the grip of an animal like Labinot made them seethe. No orders were given but the response was absolute. Though all of them could feel the onset of exhaustion, they shunned sleep or rest. They loaded up their original truck with what ammo was left and headed north for the last time.

20

As the truck growled and trundled its way over the now-familiar road, Carlisle was trying out various plans in his mind. In truth he knew that if they had been captured then no plans would be of any use. It would be a question of busking it on the day. He turned to Hardy.

'How many men do you think he's got left, Rich?'

'If Tomarzo's figures were accurate then I'd say a couple of hundred max.'

'That's about the figure I had in mind.'

'What I can't work out is the sudden rush to get back.'

'That's what I'm wondering. There must be some reason why he'd dash back. A sadistic bastard like that would have loved mopping up the remains of Khodja's men.'

The word 'sadistic' made Hardy shudder. If their two comrades were captive then he dreaded to think what state they might be in by now. Moley was cursing himself for having advised them to slow down on the trip to the ammo dump.

'If anything's happened it'll be my fault,' he said.

'It's no one's fault, Moley,' Carlisle said firmly. 'I told you all at the beginning, this is a dirty job.'

'Yeah, but . . .'

'No buts, Moley. Anyway, it'll take some good men to trouble that pair. They're probably fine. You'll see.'

Carlisle didn't believe a word of it but even a bit of false optimism was better than nothing.

The truth was stranger than any of them had guessed. Gray and Pug had been spotted dragging the body of the drunken Albanian and jamming it into the air vent. Labinot's men had guessed correctly that they would also exit from there. As they tried to escape they were knocked unconscious and that was all they remembered until they were led into the main hall of the fort.

Labinot had been radioed during the battle that two mercenaries had been captured. What prompted him to leave with such haste was the news that one of them, Pug, had killed a man with a single blow. In an instant Labinot knew he would have good sport with his new prisoners. Flush with his defeat of his old rival, he'd hotfooted back to see this fighting man in action. To spice things up, a cruel twist was introduced into the contest.

The light from the torches in the main hall blinded the two Englishmen as they had been kept chained in a darkened room until Labinot's return. There were no electric lights as the mortar attack had knocked out the generator. With the flaming brands all around them it was like a scene from medieval times.

They were led at gunpoint to the centre of the hall, which had been cleared to form a sort of arena. Then Gray was led to one end and Pug to the other. Pug was stripped to the waist, while Gray had his hands strapped behind him.

A huge peasant was brought forward. He looked Pug in the eye and snarled at him. The men all around roared and it dawned on Pug what was going to happen next. Before he had a chance to speak a weasely little man appeared and hissed, 'You beat this man your friend OK.'

'Fuck you, I'm no performing poodle – not for anyone,' growled Pug.

The little man shrugged and waved to two figures in the shadows. They came forward and dragged a brazier with them. Gray knew now what his fate would be. They took the glowing irons from the brazier and held them to his eyes. They were going to blind him.

'For fuck's sake, Pug, waste the cunt,' he yelled.

Pug nodded to his pal and stepped forward. The drunken mob that surrounded both men roared even more loudly. Huge bets were struck as they sparred around each other. Pug's opponent was vast but slow. The ex-Para nailed him with a right-hand sucker punch and he rocked to his toes. He followed this with a left upper cut and another cross, sending half the man's teeth across the makeshift ring. Pug finished him off with a vicious head-butt. The Albanian was carried off as Labinot's men ranted and raved. Drink was spilling off the tables. The torturers' eyes were still fixed on their helpless captive.

Both Pug and Gray were naive enough to think that this would bring an end to the evening's bizarre entertainment. Labinot and his cruel cohorts had other ideas.

No sooner had the first opponent been dragged away than another stepped forward. This man was slightly smaller than the last but much faster. The soldiers started to bang on their tables and more bets were struck. Pug looked over to his lifelong friend and mouthed a message. The message was not to worry. Pug would rather die in combat than see his mate suffer at the hands of these brutes.

He charged at the man opposite him, but as well as being quick this opponent fought dirty. He dodged Pug and with one hand threw pepper in his eyes and with the other delivered a mighty hook. Pug's eye closed under the impact of the blow. The other man hit him hard again and he reeled about in a blind stupor. The howling mob rose to their feet. They chanted dementedly for the destruction of the Englishman. Half blinded, Pug staggered and lurched as the Albanian whipped punch after punch into his bloodied face. His eyes were beginning to clear and he lashed out at his tormentor.

But the man could fight. Even as Pug managed to return fire he attacked even more viciously. The torturers giggled at the demise of the Englishman. They were clearly eager to press on with their hideous work. Gray squirmed in his chair and called out to Pug, urging his battered friend on.

Another fearsome punch split Pug's lip. The blood poured from his mouth and dripped down his enormous chest. Labinot, in his chair high above the carnage, pointed to Pug, then burst into maniacal laughter. He found the mercenary's pitiful state highly amusing, as did those sitting around him. They cheered on the massive Albanian. Defeat and death looked certain now. Pug dropped to one knee, but there was no referee or mandatory count in this fight. As the Albanian charged in for the kill Gray pleaded with Pug virtually for his life. Pug could see his mate's terrified face through the swirl of chanting bodies. It enraged him to see a man as brave as Gray be reduced to a pleading wreck. He stood bolt upright. The speed with which he rose, and the vast power with which he had become charged, shocked his opponent. The man hesitated and that was the last thing he ever did. Pug opened up with a barrage of punches that forced him back towards the crowd, who pushed him, semi-conscious, back into the line of fire. Pug shot out a lightning-fast right hand and killed his opponent with the single blow. In his fury he stooped down over the corpse and mashed the man's face into the flagstone floor.

Gray had seen the next opponent limbering up. He'd realized that they were playing for vital time.

Their only chance was that Carlisle would arrive like the cavalry. Though an absurdly slim chance, it was the only one they had. He shouted at his friend.

'Don't waste your strength, Pug. There's another cunt ready and waiting.'

The torturers next to Gray hit him across the face. An ugly gash opened up as they'd hit the injury he'd picked up in the mortar attack on the fort. This amused the sadistic animals and they roared with laughter. Gray became so outraged at this senseless act of cruelty that it fired him with an extraordinary burst of strength. So much so that he wriggled partly out of his bonds.

The next fighter was ready and so Pug's torment continued. But no matter how hard he was hit and butted and gouged, he wouldn't go down. Fighter after fighter pummelled him until his face became hideously distorted. His mind and body had gone a light-year beyond the frontier of normal human endurance. But he wouldn't drop. He slew every opponent and still managed to grin and wink at his pal.

'We're OK, Lenny, let them come, son, just let them come. They won't stop Pug Devaney,' he bellowed through cracked teeth and a badly gashed mouth.

His twelfth opponent entered the arena as Carlisle's team scaled the breached perimeter wall. In no time at all they had dispatched the guards and moved across to the main complex. They charged through the door and wasted the sentries with four quick bursts of their Kalashnikovs. They kicked in doors and killed anyone and everyone they came across. As they neared the main hall they could hear the frenzied shouting of the crowd.

The twelfth fighter was laying into Pug, who was badly beaten and mortally tired now. Gray knew it was close to the end. His plan was to wrench his hands free and at least take out the two torturers, who by now were practically licking their lips. A fearsome blow smashed Pug's nose halfway across his face; another opened up yet another gash on his cheekbone. His hands dropped and the Albanian bowed to his hysterical audience. He showed Pug his fist and then smashed it into his face. Pug's brain was nearly dead inside his skull and he couldn't respond. He just stood like a sacrificial animal as the second murderous punch exploded in his face. Gray pleaded with him once again – but this time for his friend to fall. To stop his cruel torment. The chanting rose to fever pitch and the crowd counted the blows it took to fell the giant Englishman. At last Gray could stand no more and wrenched his hands free. He turned on the two men who were about to blind and dismember him for the amusement of what remained of Labinot's army. It was as he grabbed the red-hot iron that Carlisle kicked in the main door to the hall.

Gray leapt at his tormentors and rammed the glowing iron into the nearest one's eye. The man died instantly. With his other hand he grabbed the second torturer and held him on the ground. He grabbed another iron and blinded the man.

'You fucker, try that for size,' he bellowed. The man screamed in agony and Gray kicked him in the groin to add to his pain.

Meanwhile Carlisle had dropped Pug's opponent with a single shot. As the mercenaries spread themselves around the hall with their rifles cocked, all the sound died. An unbelievable silence settled on the mob, who seconds earlier had been baying for blood. The stillness in the hall was surreal. Labinot looked down at the intruders. His wild eyes searched over them in disbelief. Moments earlier he had believed himself to be the leader-elect of Albania. Now death stared him in the face. He didn't move a muscle.

Gray rushed over to Pug. His friend stood transfixed in the middle of the arena. His eyes were wide open and glazed. Gray embraced him and held him as though he was a child. He whispered to him as they shuffled over to Carlisle, 'It's over, Pug. We're going home, mate. Come on, Pug, we're going home.' He repeated this over and over to the shattered fighter. As he reached Carlisle his leader stopped him.

'This place still wired, Lenny?'

'Should be. Primed and ready to blow.'

Carlisle called out to the others to get behind him. Step by step they backed towards the open main door. As they got near he called out to the Albanians.

'English?'

The weasely soldier who'd spoken earlier to Gray stepped sheepishly forward.

'A little,' he mumbled.

'Then I've got a little message for you. Tell your boss to stay where he is, OK?'

The man nodded and gave Labinot the message.

'We don't want any more trouble,' Carlisle continued. 'Just stay put and we'll leave. The whole of Albania is yours.'

Labinot beamed as he heard this in his own language. He raised his hand to Carlisle in a gesture of friendship. Carlisle saluted him in return. Then Labinot spoke to the interpreter, who relayed the message to the mercenaries.

'My leader says you are all good brave soldiers. Stay and fight with Labinot.'

Carlisle played for a bit more time. As he spoke the rest had emptied out of the main hall and Gray took the radio detonator, which was still strapped to Pug's inner thigh. He spoke over Carlisle's shoulder.

'Ready, boss.'

'OK then, get ready to move. Speed of light, Lenny,' Carlisle said, then called over to the interpreter once again. 'Tell your leader we are deeply honoured at his gracious invitation. However, we are surely not worthy. And in any case we have to go home – our tea is ready.'

The man was puzzling over the last part of the message as Carlisle backed out of the door and dashed out of the building. He dived at the open doorway and landed on the sandy earth.

'Do it, Lenny!' he yelled at Gray while still in mid-air.

Gray's finger hit the button and after the safe delay of three seconds the fort was blown to pieces. Exactly as the two men had planned, the central tower collapsed in on itself, pulling down the rest of the fort, and Labinot and his men were sent to hell, where they belonged. Elsa rose from the ground and dusted herself off. She walked to Carlisle and hugged him.

'Now my people can be free. I can never repay you, Peter.'

Carlisle said nothing. He gazed at the remains of the once mighty mountain stronghold. He turned to his men and thanked them with all his heart. Under the starry Albanian sky they filed out of the fort. It was the last time they would move as one unit.

Within minutes the truck was rumbling south again. Moley was at the wheel and Carlisle and Hardy were in the cab. The rest were flat out in the back. Carlisle spoke to Moley.

'Let's get back to the dump. We'll load up with HE and come back here and finish off the hangar over there. It'll be a tricky job but that stuff's got to be buried where it is.'

'Check, Pete. Shouldn't be that difficult. And then what?'

'Hang around for a week and see that no other fucker rears his ugly head and then, brave comrades, it's home.'

'Home,' mused Hardy. 'Christ, I forgot I had one.'

'That's the modern mercenary life for you,' joked

Carlisle. 'You see, a week's domestic bliss and you'll be straining at the leash to get back.'

'I doubt it,' was Hardy's flat reply.

Though Carlisle's remarks to his men had only been in jest it saddened him to be losing soldiers of their calibre. They were the finest men he'd known. He owed his life to two of them, Hardy and Lane. You didn't easily cut such comrades out of your life. And then there was Elsa . . . He was addicted to her. He never got entangled as a rule; these missions were difficult enough without such complications. Kate his wife was a subject he drove out of his mind on these missions. To think of her back home would only weaken his resolve.

He remembered the stories of the SAS in Oman. Some bright spark had had the idea that 'our lads in the desert' would experience a great boost to their morale if audio tapes of their nearest and dearest were ferried out to them. The result was whole platoons sitting in tears as little Johnny related stories of his first swim in the sea or little Susie told of her first day at school. Better, Carlisle knew, to separate the two worlds. Kate was his wife. She belonged back in West Hampstead. And so did half of him. His problem was that the other half belonged with Elsa. Just how was he going to readjust? He was pondering this question when the truck pulled off the track and rolled up to the ammo dump.

He was about to find Elsa when Hardy called him with urgency in his voice.

'Pete, you'd better get over here a minute. We've got a problem.'

'What's up, Rich?' he asked.

Before Hardy could answer the impassioned shouts of Gray filled the silent clearing.

'Pug! Pug!'

Gray was holding his comrade by the shoulders and his face was pressed against his. He was pleading with his friend to answer him. But Pug had taken one punch too many. The man's brain was scrambled. As he stood gazing blankly ahead of him Carlisle could see clearly that his fine blue eyes saw nothing. His strong Irish heart beat blood to a mind that would never function properly again. The terrible punishment he'd endured had destroyed him. Even as Gray held him he collapsed shuddering where he lay.

Gray could contain himself no longer. He hugged the fallen giant and kissed him as his tears gripped on to Pug's disfigured face. Then he stepped back and realized the convulsions had ended. There in front of them was all that was left of Anthony Devaney. The sheer strength of the man would not allow his body to die. Yet the brain was dead. His handsome dark face would never smile or snarl again. He would never joke or banter. He now occupied a world as dark as outer space.

When Gray looked up at the others there was a silence that seemed to last longer than a lifetime. Carlisle could read Gray's tortured mind. Pug was a fighting man, a born soldier. What would life mean for him back home? A weary journey through long-term institutions. A husk of a man who dribbled in his food. A once-proud warrior not even able to wipe his own arse. Gray's heart was broken. He looked with tear-filled eyes at Carlisle, who nodded to his unspoken request.

They laid their bodies on Pug, embracing him more than restricting him. Then Gray held his hand over the mouth and nostrils of his lifelong friend. The struggle was a mighty one. The man's body was on automatic. He struggled violently to survive. He thrashed and fought like a wild bull, but his compassionate executioners would not, could not relent. A calm descended on them as they rose and moved away from the dead man. They had transported him to a better world than he would ever know on earth.

21

Carlisle slept with Elsa that night. Not for sex; it was comfort he needed. As he woke, her beautiful eyes were close to his.

'Are you all right, darling?' she whispered tenderly.

'I don't have a great deal of choice,' he answered. 'If I crack they all crack. And that wouldn't do, would it?'

This calm understatement moved Elsa greatly. She knew now, having seen this man endure the most terrible blows with such stoic heroism, why she loved him. She knew she would never meet his like again. It was a bitter-sweet feeling because she knew they would part soon and probably for ever.

'What do we do now, my love?'

'We bury Pug with all the decency and dignity we can muster. Then we go home.'

A look of horror had spread over her face.

'We can't bury him here. The ground isn't sanctified,' she said.

'Elsa, we can't cart Pug's body round the country like so much scrap iron.'

'There is a church in my village. It would be a suitable resting-place.'

'How far is your village?'

'Thirty kilometres from here.'

Carlisle nodded and just before midday the men loaded Pug's body on to the truck and moved off. It was a solemn journey over rough, twisting mountain tracks. Moley was at the wheel and Hardy was in the cab with Carlisle and Elsa.

'How's Lenny doing, Rich?' Carlisle asked.

'Pretty bad, Pete. Don't think he's gonna be the same again. Him and Pug go back a long way.'

'He'll mend – we all do,' said Carlisle. Hardy knew that Carlisle's was the voice of experience but he wondered about Gray. He was beginning to rant.

'He keeps going on about Tomarzo, Pete. Saying it's all his fault. Keeps calling him a fucking Nazi.'

'Shouldn't listen too closely. He's got to blame someone if he wants to keep his sanity. It might as well be that piece of shit as anyone.'

This seemed reasonable enough and no one raised the matter again. The truck rolled on through the dramatic mountain country and around mid-afternoon they entered Elsa's village.

'Welcome to my home, gentlemen. This is the village of Vlora,' she said wearily.

The place was small, the population couldn't have been more than two hundred. It was so well concealed that they had come upon it almost unwittingly. It seemed this was the way with this country. The whitewashed houses were huddled close together, and the village lay on various levels because of the rocky nature of the place. Very slowly the inhabitants came out to greet the mercenaries in a shy but orderly way. The men were all farming types. Their clothes were simple and their faces red and weather-beaten. The women were for the most part stout and maternal. Most wore shawls. The children, mainly barefoot, were excited and ran in giddy circles around their mothers' skirts.

Elsa walked forward and embraced a middle-aged woman. Her features told Carlisle she was Elsa's mother. Then a collection of people surrounded her, and Elsa said, 'Gentlemen, this is my mother, Saranda, my sisters Dana and Arbana and my brothers Ardian, Shpat and Hegran.'

Carlisle made no comment but wondered to himself why Elsa had made no reference to her father, or for that matter where he might be.

When greetings had been exchanged Elsa explained to her family the tragic reason for their visit.

Within an hour her brothers had dug a grave in the churchyard, situated at the northern end of the village. The church itself was a simple whitewashed building that seemed to have been converted from a mosque to a Christian place of worship.

The men took Pug's body, wrapped in a rough woollen blanket, from the truck. They carried him through the village, passing the solemn villagers on the way. The priest, an old, bearded man, stooped and kissed the forehead of the fallen warrior. An Albanian flag was fetched and Elsa turned to Carlisle and said, 'They wish to bury him in the flag because he died fighting to free our country.'

Carlisle said nothing but shot a glance to Gray.

'Yeah, fine,' was Gray's simple reply.

Wrapped in the twin-eagled Albanian flag, Pug was lowered into the grave. The priest chanted a strange litany over the corpse and when he'd finished Elsa turned to Carlisle. He responded by offering a short but moving prayer to the dead man and that was that. They walked back to Elsa's house and sat in gloomy silence.

Within minutes Elsa's mother had produced steaming plates of food.

'We call it *fli*. It's only simple peasant food but . . .' said Elsa.

'Thank you, Elsa,' Carlisle replied. He knew she was trying to cheer them along but it was better to let them sit in silence. It was their way. The men picked through the meal, which was a mixture of pastry, eggs and yoghurt. It tasted good but they could barely finish it. Carlisle knew that it must have cost Elsa's family a lot to feed all these extra mouths. It was wrong to sit in the home of these simple people with such little gratitude. Carlisle asked Elsa to thank her family for everything and they left, Elsa with them.

Outside, Carlisle was about to say something when Elsa cut him short.

'They understand, they have suffered also,' she said.

There was a melancholy note in her voice that made Carlisle wonder what she meant. She wasn't talking about the normal trials of life, that was for sure. Elsa's absent father sprang into his mind.

'We didn't meet your father today. Is he working away?' he asked.

'He was . . .' It was no good – her lip started to tremble and she shook her head.

Carlisle thought he knew the answer.

'Was he one of the men we saw Khodja's men execute?'

'Probably,' she answered finally.

Carlisle put his arm around her shoulder and they drove back to the ammo dump in silence. There was nothing anyone could say.

Something was playing on Carlisle's mind. He'd worked out roughly where on the map the village of Vlora might be. It would coincide with the point indicated by a question mark on the map on the *Cassandra*. Now wasn't the time to raise the issue; Elsa had enough on her mind. But if Oppenshaff had the village marked on his map then he must have a damn good reason.

They were back at the ammo dump by early evening. Morale had fallen through the floor. Carlisle addressed the team and told them the plan. It was obvious to him, though, that Gray was in no shape to go over the old ground of Labinot's territory. He knew he would have to find a good excuse to leave him behind, for Gray was a proud man. He took him aside after the briefing and said, 'Lenny, I want you to take the other truck and get back to Salonika. I don't trust Tomarzo, so keep an eye on him, can you? We'll mop up here and be back within three days. OK?' In fact there was a glimmer of truth in it. Tomarzo held the purse-strings and Carlisle's pot was nearly empty. He had enough dollars left to pay for a hotel to rest in for a night and then to get them back to England.

Gray was no fool, but although he realized Carlisle was giving him an early bath he was in no mood to argue. He answered in a weary voice, 'Check, boss. I might as well go now. I can be back there in four hours.'

In the morning Carlisle washed in the spring. The water was clean and pure. It felt almost like a baptism as he splashed in its invigorating flow. Soon this whole bloody mess would be over. And the sooner the better. He called the men round and they loaded up the weapons and ammunition and left within the hour.

The heat was rising and Carlisle opened the passenger door as they drove north. He turned to Hardy, who was driving, and said, 'Keep a sharp eye out, Rich. There might be snipers around when we get up there. We don't know for sure that was all Labinot's strength in that hall.'

Nothing looked to have survived when they got to the ruin of Labinot's fort. The building itself was no more than a heap of rubble, in and around which were strewn hundreds of bodies, now buzzing with flies. Fierce-looking eagles were busy cleaning up the rotting bodies, which, in the summer heat, gave off a disgusting stench.

'Let's get this over with, lads,' said Carlisle.

Moley looked over the hangar and wired up the structure to blow without creating too much down-blast. It was a difficult job, for it had to be precise. Three hours later he called over to Carlisle, 'Ready, boss. Let's get clear.'

Except for Moley, they all stood at a distance of about fifty yards, and he pressed the detonator. The blast was deafening and smothered the sniper's shot that smashed through Moley's shoulder. He screamed with the pain, but the others could hear nothing over the blast and when he rolled in the dust they assumed he was larking around. The sniper opened up again and hit Moley a second time. This time everyone heard it loud and clear. They threw themselves behind what cover they could find and looked for the direction of the shot. For a few brief seconds there was nothing. Carlisle called to Lane and Hardy.

'I'm going to draw his fire, lads. Eyes peeled and waste the fucker.'

They had no time to warn him not to. In an instant Carlisle rose and dashed across the compound. The sniper opened up again. His cover was blown and before he had a chance to take another pop Hardy had nailed him. They walked over to the source of fire. It was a boy of twelve or thirteen. Hardy's round had torn open a vast hole where his chest had been. Soon he would be a tender snack for the circling birds.

'Let's get out of here,' said Carlisle.

After a search of the area they found no sign of a living soul.

Moley insisted he wasn't badly hurt. But Lane, who tended to him in the rear of the truck, wasn't so sure. The first shot had grazed his shoulder-blade but otherwise had done no real harm. The second shot, though, had hit him in the lower chest and smashed three ribs. Lane told him firmly to take it easy until they got him back to Salonika.

As the truck pulled up by the ruins of Khodja's fort Moley was the first out and lugged a two-hundred-pound load of HE as he went. Lane could only stare in amazement at the man.

Khodja's fortress, or what was left of it, shimmered in the late-afternoon heat. Tiny rodents darted in and out of the piles of gigantic broken stones. The ubiquitous eagles were circling above and plunging down occasionally to feed.

'We'll blow it anyway,' ordered Carlisle, then wandered off to look at a tree thirty yards south of the smashed entrance. He recognized the thick, gnarled trunk from the photo he'd been given. It was where his friend had met his dreadful end.

It still pained him greatly to think that Mike Greenwood's corpse had been butchered and then not even buried, dumped, in all probability, like a bin bag. It occurred to him that some sign of him might still be close by – a cap badge or anything. He decided to look in the nearby pine grove.

A brief search revealed nothing, and the task was beginning to depress Carlisle profoundly. He turned to head back to the others when a powerful arm wrapped round his neck. Adrenalin raced like a bullet through his body. Out of the corner of his eye he caught the flash of the knife blade. The best he could do was take the thrust on his forearm. His scream of pain was heard by the others and they ran fully armed into the grove.

Before they got there Carlisle had grasped his attacker's wrist and twisted it with all his super-charged strength, sending the knife flying through the air. Still holding the man's wrist, he whipped his body round and brought his knee up into his belly. Then he dropped him, winded, on to the ground, where the others covered him with their weapons. Further off, in a hollow, were a dozen huddled figures. How different beaten men looked. They snivelled and whined as they walked forward with their arms held high in the air. What they didn't know was that Carlisle and Hardy recognized at least two of them. They were the ones who had castrated the wretched peasants – one of whom was probably Elsa's father. The man who'd just tried to kill Carlisle now had cracked front teeth and a diagonal scar over his left eye. But there was no mistaking him.

'Remember this one, Rich?' Carlisle called over to

Hardy, who nodded slowly, never taking his eyes off the man. Carlisle called Elsa over.

'Find out what this lot are up to,' he said.

Elsa broke into Albanian and there followed an animated dialogue. There was much shrugging of shoulders. The men's voices had a pleading tone about them.

'They say they're nothing to do with Khodja,' said Elsa. 'He was a wicked man and they thought you were from his fortress. They want to apologize for the attack.'

'I'll bet they do,' said Carlisle with a stony face. 'Ask them how they know there are still some soldiers up at the fortress.'

The men responded a little more confidently. They clearly thought they were fooling the Englishman. In fact he was toying with them; not because he was a cruel man but because he loathed these creatures.

'They say they're not sure. They say if they do see any, though, they'll wipe them off the face of the earth.'

'Do you believe them, Elsa?'

Carlisle was curious to know how much insight she possessed.

'No, they're lying,' she answered without the slightest hesitation. Carlisle was impressed.

'The one closest to you – see him?' he said.

Elsa turned her head slightly. The man with the cracked teeth grinned nervously at her.

'Yes.'

'He killed your father.'

Elsa trembled and then steadied herself. Then she raised her Browning automatic. The man's mouth gaped open. Her bullet went through his open mouth and out the back of his head. The remainder of the prisoners were dispatched by the others. The last of Khodja's men were dead.

Moley touched the detonator and the last remnants of the fortress turned to dust. The sun was setting as they moved away. It was dark by the time they reached the shore of Lake Ohrid for the last time. The fishermen were wary in the extreme, but eventually Elsa managed to persuade them they had nothing to fear. After haggling briefly they agreed to exchange the truck for a crossing to Ohrid. The lights of the medieval town blinked softly at them. They had no arms now. All evidence of their activities was back at the hidden dump or blown to pieces along with Khodja's fortress. It seemed strange to Carlisle not to feel the dead weight of the trusty 9mm auto drag on his right shoulder. For the first time in a month he felt free.

22

The hot jets of the hotel shower played over Carlisle's taut body. He wanted the dust of the Albanian killing fields off him. The team's motivation had flagged with the death of Pug. That and the relentless pressure of the campaign had drained them. No one would be out clubbing tonight.

It was midnight as Carlisle joined Elsa on the hotel balcony. He kissed her tenderly and sat looking over the lake. From nowhere she pulled out a bottle of Bushmills and placed it gently on his lap.

Carlisle's eyes filled with tears. In his present state of mind such kindness overwhelmed him.

'I'm going to bed, darling,' Elsa whispered in his ear. 'You drink and rest. It's time you were alone for a while.'

As Carlisle looked at her vanishing into the bedroom he believed in miracles. How could she have known of his profound need for silence and introspection after such missions? Leaving this woman wasn't going to be easy. If indeed it was going to be possible.

He poured the brackish malt into his glass and

rinsed his mouth with a huge first gulp. It surged into his body, warming and insulating him against the world.

As he drank, Carlisle thought of Mike Greenwood. The man was a rare brave genius. He had run through his friend's life and his cruelly premature end, as well as a few more stories, by the time he was nearing the end of the bottle. He at least had his memories and he was thankful for that. But he'd give his right arm to bring Mike back. And Pug. And God knows who else who was going to die on such missions. But if these bitter-sweet recollections did nothing else then they sharpened his appetite for life. After all, it might be Peter Carlisle who became a memory tomorrow. As he thought this Elsa gave a sigh and then a gentle moan as she turned in her sleep. Just the sound of her, just the smell of her, and he was aroused.

'Shh,' he called softly, then stole silently to bed.

The difference a shower and a good night's sleep made was unbelievable. The next day they all looked ten years younger. The sun was well up by the time they crammed the tables for breakfast.

'Righto, lads, we drive back down to Salonika and pick Lenny up. Then we can drive or fly back home,' Carlisle told the team.

The vote was to fly. They'd all seen enough of roads in the last few weeks. With their spirits a little higher they rumbled out of Ohrid in a Peugeot estate car procured by Moley. It was mid-afternoon.

It was seven p.m. when they reached Salonika. The harbour was empty. The *Cassandra* had gone, and the triangle of shimmering water looked clean but bare without her. Otherwise the town looked much the same. With its bars and restaurants it looked bustling and urbane after the bleakness of Albania.

'Wonder where Lenny is,' mused Lane.

'He won't be far,' said Carlisle. 'Come on, we'll check into the hotel. He should be hanging around . . .'

'In the bar,' Hardy completed the sentence. They all laughed.

They scoured the bars around the harbour but found no sign of Gray. He'd booked out of the hotel the day before but left no forwarding address.

'Well, he wouldn't leave an address. He's scarpered off home, I reckon,' said Hardy. 'Losing Pug like that. He's just had a bellyful of it.'

'Maybe,' said Carlisle and then turned sharply to Elsa. 'I think we'll pay your old boss a visit. Lenny must be around there somewhere.'

It wasn't like Carlisle to fret but he sensed immediately that something was badly wrong.

They got a taxi to Tomarzo's apartment. It looked empty. Elsa kept guard while Carlisle picked the lock in less than a minute.

'Wonder if he's taken a little cruise with Oppenshaff?' he whispered to Elsa once they were inside.

'I doubt it. Their arrangement was for Tomarzo to deliver a number of priceless art treasures. Those are still where my people hid them.'

'How do you know that?'

'Let's just say I do,' Elsa said, smiling enigmatically, then went on, 'That would be construed as a serious failure by Oppenshaff. And I don't think Mr Oppenshaff is a man who tolerates serious failure.'

'No,' replied Carlisle. 'I think we'll see what old Nicomedes has hidden away under his bed.'

They moved quietly through the darkened apartment. It was suffused with the smell of expensive perfumes. Carlisle took a pencil torch from his shirt pocket, and shone it over artefacts, canvases and ordinary household objects. Nothing. They were about to leave when he turned and shone the torch over the main room once again.

On the far wall was a large canvas of a Napoleonic battle scene. It was slightly skewed.

'It's not like our Nicomedes to be so sloppy,' said Carlisle.

He lifted the painting from the wall. A panel gave way and they stepped into a completely empty room. There was a musty smell like an antique shop. There were the faint marks of picture frames on the walls. And there were tiny spots of blood on the white walls.

Carlisle's heart began to race. He'd seen those patterns of blood before. Back in Iran at the hands of sadistic torturers. Elsa could see the alarm on his taut features.

'Where do you think that blood came from, Peter?'

'I don't think Tomarzo cut himself shaving. Shall we go?'

The taxi pulled up at the hotel as Hardy wandered out, grinning broadly. He saw the look on Carlisle's face and waved to him and called out, 'Don't worry about Lenny, boss. He left a message at reception. Apparently the new girl forgot to mention it.'

Hardy took out a tattered piece of paper. It read: 'Pete and the lads, Got fed up waiting, see you all back at HQ. Yours, Len.'

Carlisle felt a wave of relief. Had the message been longer or the paper a bit more respectable then he would have been suspicious. But the short note on crumpled paper was Gray's style.

'Shall we celebrate, chaps?' he beamed.

It was nearly one-thirty in the morning and they were sitting at a table outside a busy bar on the waterfront. The atmosphere was friendly and relaxed. Even Moley, as he swigged his tenth bottle of Tuborg Export, seemed at ease. Next to the table was a newspaper vending machine. Carlisle was leaning back in his chair, letting the cooling breeze from the harbour flow over him. As his eyes rested idly on the heap of papers under the Perspex cover he suddenly sat bolt upright. Under a maze of Greek type was a blurry photo. It showed a body mostly covered by a sheet, with an arm sticking out. Carlisle put in two coins and pulled the top paper out.

'Elsa! What the hell does that say?' he said as he pointed to the headlines above the photo.

'A mutilated body has been found in the harbour,' she said.

'Carlisle passed the paper over the table to Hardy and Moley. Their eyes scanned it briefly, then both men looked at Carlisle and nodded gravely. There was no need to say a thing. The arm in the photo was tattooed. 'Lenny – Joyce. Norwich 1993,' it read.

'Let's go,' said Carlisle, and drained his glass of Metaxa.

He made a phone call from the hotel foyer. The tone rang twice and an oily voice answered. It belonged to Garvan, the recruiting sergeant.

'Yes?'

'Carlisle, code doc/eagle 898.'

'Reading you, Mr Carlisle.'

'Mission complete. Return to HQ. ETA 0600 hours, 24/8/94.'

'Thank you, Mr Carlisle.'

The phone went dead.

23

Thirty-six hours earlier Gray had been sitting in the harbourside bar the group had just left. He'd arrived in Salonika in a very depressed state. After wandering around for a while he'd thought of going to the Apollo Casino to sort out the money they'd robbed him of. Somehow he didn't have the heart for it. Instead he found a bar and, with no one to talk to, drank solidly for over two hours.

He wandered back to the hotel and got his things together. On the spur of the moment he'd decided to make his way home alone. He left a note with the young girl behind reception.

His train wasn't due for an hour. He floated off to the same bar again. He'd got through another five beers when Tomarzo and Agron spotted him. He could barely make them out. He stared through bleary eyes as Tomarzo greeted him in his usual sickly polite way. Had he been sober he'd have stayed put. Instead he accepted the invitation to Tomarzo's apartment.

Tomarzo started by plying him with simple questions about how the mission had gone and so on. He minced around and filled Gray's glass as soon as it emptied. As Gray's answers became more terse under the influence of the alcohol, Tomarzo grew increasingly irritated.

'What was in Labinot's fort? What exactly did you see?'

'Fuck all. Fuck all there, mate,' stuttered Gray drunkenly. Then he added, 'Oh, oh yeah, a load of heavy concrete containers came in. Just a load of concrete.'

He was beginning to pass out but Tomarzo had to know if anything else had been found in the vanquished fort. He knew what the concrete concealed. Enriched nuclear material. That was a problem he could deal with. But if the Byzantine treasures had been in Labinot's clutches then by now they would surely have been destroyed.

That would be a catastrophe for Tomarzo. His personal master plan had relied on the sale of those treasures. Now this drunken Englishman was the only source of information. He was growing dangerously impatient. With Agron to hand, he dared to seize Gray's collar.

'Mr Gray, let me explain . . .'

'Concrete, mate. Just a load of fucking concrete,' Gray mumbled, too drunk now to be worried by the Greek's overfamiliarity.

'Stop it! You idiot!' yelled Tomarzo. His face was an inch from Gray's and it was burning with rage.

In the miasma of drunken images drifting through

Gray's brain the photo in the room with the Nazi regalia kept returning.

'You!' he blurted out. 'I've seen that photo of you. Or your dad or whoever it fucking is. You're a fucking Nazi. That's what you are. You had my mate killed . . .'

Agron's mighty hand slammed down on the back of Gray's neck.

Gray came to in handcuffs in a room that was a replica of the 'Nazi room' in Labinot's fort. This time, though, the photo of Tomarzo was walking around. The Greek was in the full dress uniform of the dreaded SS. He was strutting round the room and screaming at Gray. But the battered Englishman could only hear him in snatches.

'Albania is my inheritance . . . the rest of the Balkans will follow . . . you people meddled after the war . . . then the new order . . .'

Gray lapsed once again into unconsciousness. By the time he'd come round again Tomarzo had calmed down.

'Leonard,' he purred, 'I don't want to be hard on you. I know you to be an excellent soldier. Your commander Carlisle has always spoken well of you. You could join me. Tomorrow will be . . .'

'Tomarzo, come here a minute.'

Gray's voice was weak and sounded strained. Tomarzo guessed he was going to crack. As he bent closer Gray spat in his face. Agron stepped forward and wiped the phlegm from his master's face. He rolled the handkerchief in a ball and rammed it into Gray's mouth. Then they sealed his mouth with parcel tape.

Agron walked casually into the main room and returned with a paintbrush. Tomarzo nodded and the Albanian calmly proceeded to coat Gray's eyeballs with paint stripper.

They tortured him for over eight hours, every now and again reviving him so that he could be interrogated on the Byzantine art treasures. What Tomarzo never suspected was that Gray was telling the truth. He'd never even heard of them.

By nine in the morning Gray was dead. They dumped his body into a wide sewer pipe, along which it inched towards the harbour until by midday it was floating by the quay. A German tourist spotted it and fainted.

Tomarzo was beside himself. He decided to travel to Kosovo. He'd hire some mercenaries there and risk the dash into Albania himself. In any case, with the warlords and their armies destroyed the main danger was gone.

It was worth the risk because he had a hunch. The hunch was the question mark he himself had drawn on Oppenshaff's map. Vlora. Elsa's village.

24

At eight in the morning the Peugeot estate headed south out of Salonika and towards the main road to Athens. Carlisle turned to the team and said, 'We're in deep shit, lads. We've got no arms, no money and a very dangerous job ahead.'

'Sounds like good odds to me,' growled Moley as they raced south. He spoke for all of them. Gray would not go unavenged. What was left of the dirty half dozen had made their minds up on that score.

'Turn her round, Moley,' said Carlisle. 'We should be able to creep back and sniff around. I get the feeling those cunts think they've shaken us. The message back to HQ will confirm that.'

Hardy looked puzzled.

'How will they know that you've confirmed mission OK with HQ?'

'My hunch is that our friend Garvan will tell them. Remember him?'

They all remembered the recruiting sergeant. They'd all sat in his smoky office in Tooley Street at some time. They all despised the man.

'Garvan! I don't follow,' said Moley as he wrenched the Peugeot round and sped back towards Salonika. 'What the fuck has that queer cunt got to do with anything?'

'Queer cunt's the connection in this case. Because some queer cunt has set us up. The same queer cunt who gave Tomarzo a security clearance higher than Mount Everest and is going to squeak to them that we've cleared out. And the only queer cunt that knows we've gone is Garvan. I phoned him last night. So let's go back and see what's what.'

They crawled back into the town along minor roads. By midnight the Peugeot was parked in a shadowy part of the quayside. At three the *Cassandra* glided imperiously into the harbour.

'Boss, I think you had it right,' whispered Hardy.

The vast, cream-coloured yacht was anchoring as a taxi pulled up at the quay. Two figures sat inside watching the beautiful boat in her gentle manoeuvres. One was Garvan.

'OK, boys, this is "go" on my command. Let's get ready.'

At the sound of a launch approaching, the taxi doors opened and Garvan's podgy figure rolled out. He pointed to the yacht and the man next to him nodded. The launch was close now and Carlisle yelled, 'Go!'

The Peugeot pulled up between the two waiting men and the launch. They all leapt out. 'Garvan!' roared Carlisle as he grabbed him.

'What are you doing here?' squealed Garvan.

'I'm going to the party and so are you.'

With this they pulled the two men on to the launch, which was just tying up, quickly overpowered the crew and took their automatic weapons from them.

'Just do your work,' Elsa hissed at one of the crew as the launch got underway.

'Have you gone mad?' Garvan protested.

'Say one more word and I'll kill you, do you understand?' growled Carlisle.

Garvan nodded.

Carlisle was in no mood for monkey business. The whole thing had unfolded in front of him. How could he have not seen it? 'Your pal here, Garvan – not interested in fine art by any chance, is he?'

'That's got nothing to do with you.'

Carlisle held the silenced CZ to Garvan's ear. The fat man shuddered and answered meekly in the affirmative.

'I thought so,' said Carlisle with a glassy look in his eye.

'You!' he called over to the other man. 'Come here.'

The man approached nervously. Carlisle eyed him with undisguised hostility.

'You plan to cut Tomarzo out of the deal, am I right?'

The man looked nervously at Garvan. Again Carlisle shouted at him, 'Am I right?'

The man, who'd not spoken, nodded slowly. Carlisle shot him in the face and kicked him into the harbour.

'Sorry, Garvan, but I haven't got time to waste finding out just how rotten your associates are.'

The launch tied up to the *Cassandra*. The crew did as Carlisle told them. The door to the main cabin burst open and Oppenshaff rose to greet his most unwelcome visitors.

'Well, gentlemen, you have me at some disadvantage. You see, I had hoped you'd all be dead by now. But alas no, and that's about all there is to it.'

'Sit down, Oppenshaff,' barked Carlisle.

'At your service, sir,' wheezed the elderly American as he flopped down into an armchair. 'Now I guess you boys are going to kill me but before you get to work I'd be obliged if you'd take a drink with me. Can't abide drinking by myself. Never could.'

'Bushmills,' said Carlisle. 'Nothing for my boys.'

Oppenshaff rose again and shuffled to the bar. He poured the malt with the same eager delight Carlisle remembered from before.

'Garvan?'

The recruiting sergeant shook his head.

'How about that fella you were going to bring – what was he called? Harris, was that it?'

'Ask him,' Garvan said acidly as he nodded at Carlisle.

'Mr Harris is fishing in the harbour. I wasted him,' said Carlisle.

'You, sir, are a fine judge of character,' said

Oppenshaff with genuine admiration. 'Why, planned to kill your good friend Garvan here. Now ain't that something, Garvan? Old Harris was gonna plug you after the deal was settled.'

Garvan's face showed obvious alarm.

'Ain't you gonna thank Mr Carlisle here? Why, he's given you a good three minutes more life, sir. So far anyway,' he grinned. 'And that from a man you planned to see exterminated out there in them mountains, yes, sir.'

Carlisle was looking at Oppenshaff as he raised the CZ. He could see Garvan squirm out of the corner of his eye. He blasted a bloody patch in the middle of the recruiting sergeant's chest, then smiled at the American and dropped the handgun.

'OK then, and purely for the record, tell us the rest,' he said.

'The rest, sir, is rather complicated. You see, all the guys you wasted had planned to do just that to you. But all for different reasons. Take Tomarzo. Why, his daddy did a whole lot of killing out here in the last war. Now he thinks that you guys have robbed him of his rightful inheritance. Ain't that kooky?'

Oppenshaff grinned mischievously. There was something infectious about the man's cheek. He started to go on but Carlisle interrupted.

'What, precisely, is your interest in the art treasures of Albania?'

'Two billion dollars,' said the American coolly.

The figure staggered everyone present. Carlisle guessed what it was about.

'Because no one has ever seen them. Am I right?' he asked.

'Correct in every particular, sir. Not the Getty, nor the . . . well, in short, no one. And now I do believe you're going to kill me, and it's getting rather late.' His eyes bored into Carlisle's, almost pleading.

Carlisle gave the signal to move out, and they backed their way to the door.

'I'm afraid we can't oblige you there, Mr Oppenshaff. You'll have to join the ranks of Getty and the rest of them. You'll never see those treasures either. Goodbye.'

As the launch moved off, Hardy looked quizzically at Carlisle.

'Why, Pete?'

'Why indeed, Rich. Let's just say that death, in a weird sort of way, would be a mercy to Oppenshaff and I'm all out of mercy.'

'I still don't follow.'

'Don't worry about it. Trust me. Anyway we've got other fish to fry.'

25

The dash to the border was frantic, for Carlisle knew he was racing against time.

'Tomarzo will think he's got a clear hand. He's bound to nose around now the big boys are out of it,' he told the team.

'Nose around – where?' asked Hardy. 'Everything's been taken out.'

'Not quite everything,' answered Carlisle as he glanced in Elsa's direction.

'I don't know what you mean,' she said.

'I think, in fact I know, you do,' came Carlisle's angry response.

'He'll never find them!' she protested.

'But he'll find your village. It was marked on Oppenshaff's map. Haven't your family suffered enough?'

Elsa's wild eyes flashed at Carlisle. She knew she had no choice but to go with him.

'Drive, Moley,' she shouted.

There was only HE left at their ammo dump and there was no time to look for the other one. They loaded up and set off for Vlora. When they got there, Elsa chased around frantically, telling the villagers only what they needed to know, and within minutes people and possessions were packed and the village was empty.

'Not like the films, eh, Moley?' joked Hardy. 'If this was the *Magnificent Seven* that lot would have got the old pitchforks and the lot out. Remember it?'

'No,' murmured Moley. He was fiddling with fuses and detonators. Elsa called him over.

'Quick, the church,' she said. They rushed over to the building with all the HE they could carry. As they ran they heard Lane call that Tomarzo was in sight.

Once inside the simple white building Elsa ripped up a mat near the altar. Under it was a trapdoor. She yanked this up, revealing a shaft some thirty feet deep.

'Down there is a blastproof chamber. That is where they are hidden,' she said.

'Wire up the church, Moley. We haven't got any choice,' said Carlisle.

Lane called out to them again.

'Better get up here, Pete, they're pretty close now.'

Everyone took up position. With only fifty rounds between them it was as well they had surprise on their side. Tomarzo had rustled together ten of the most desperate soldiers Carlisle had ever seen.

'Whites of their eyes, lads,' he hissed. They opened up at about twenty yards and took six of them out at once. But that was their ammo nearly spent. They waited for a counter but the familiar rattle of gunfire never came. Instead two stun grenades flew over.

When they came to, their hands were bound and Tomarzo was looming over them.

'Nice to see you back with us, gentlemen,' he said, laughing. 'And now if I might trouble you for the whereabouts of my inheritance?'

'Don't know what you're talking about,' sneered Carlisle.

'Don't you? Perhaps Agron can help you.'

He signalled to the giant Albanian. Agron started to beat Carlisle savagely with his fists. Carlisle winced as blow after sickening blow rained down on him. At last Elsa could bear no more, and yelled in Albanian, 'Leave him – he doesn't know.'

Tomarzo's eyes shone an even brighter blue.

'Then perhaps you do. Agron, proceed.'

Agron was even more brutal with the woman. He smashed her about the head and her beautiful face was soon a hideous mask of blood and swellings. He began to rip her clothes off. Moley couldn't stand it.

'The church, it's in the church, you fuckers.'

'Stop!' Tomarzo beamed in triumph. 'I thought that would be far more difficult. You gentlemen have perhaps had enough. Once we have inspected your claim we will be back to put you out of your misery. Agron!' Tomarzo signalled for the Albanian to stay with them. The rest of his motley band joined him.

In the dying light of the afternoon all eyes except Agron's were on the church. They shuffled around the building at first but greed drove them on. After a minute Carlisle shouted to Moley, 'Blast them!'

'I can't, Pete. The detonator's in the front pocket.'

Agron had sprung to his feet at this exchange. So did Carlisle and his men. They circled the brute like hunting dogs. With their hands still bound they were reduced to literally baring their teeth. Before Agron could raise the alarm or move, Elsa had picked the detonator from Moley's pocket. She backed up to him and he grabbed it as Agron began to shout. A millisecond later the church erupted and the sound seemed to be rushing from his now gaping mouth.

As usual, Moley had done an expert job. The church had been turned into a cloud of white chips which blew in a snow cloud all around them. Before the dust settled they knew they had to kill Agron. The Albanian had collected himself by now and snarled at the pack.

'All at once,' Carlisle roared. 'Kick, bite, do anything you can.'

Then he dived at Agron. Their last enemy laughed hideously as he hurled his desperate attacker high in the air. Then the others rushed at him. He repulsed them, then grabbed Elsa, who writhed in his monstrous grip until her neck snapped like an icicle.

Moley was on his feet again and dived straight at Agron. A scream split the air and a fatal gash opened up in the Albanian's neck as Moley sank his teeth deep into the flesh. In that single moment of shock Agron paused. Hardy scrambled to his feet and let fly a deadly kick to the stricken man's temple. Agron rocked and Lane closed in with a savage kick to the groin. The man fell and was kicked and stamped to death within seconds.

It took them a short while to get untied. They walked over to the church. Tomarzo's body lay crushed under the debris. Half his face was caved in; the other half was unmarked. The unscathed blue eye stared up at them. It glinted in the sharp rays of the setting sun like a cold, bright sapphire. They turned away. Then there was a strange sound behind them. Everyone turned at once to see an eagle rush up into the air. In its fearsome beak was the remaining blue eye of Nicomedes Tomarzo.

OTHER TITLES IN SERIES FROM 22 BOOKS

Available now at newsagents and booksellers
or use the order form provided

continued overleaf . . .

*   *   *

All at £4.99 net

All 22 Books are available at your bookshop, or can be ordered from:

22 Books
Mail Order Department
Little, Brown and Company
Brettenham House
Lancaster Place
London WC2E 7EN

Alternatively, you may fax your order to the above address. Fax number: 0171 911 8100.

Payments can be made by cheque or postal order, payable to Little, Brown and Company (UK), or by credit card (Visa/ Access). Do not send cash or currency. UK, BFPO and Eire customers, please allow 75p per item for postage and packing, to a maximum of £7.50. Overseas customers, please allow £1 per item.

While every effort is made to keep prices low, it is sometimes necessary to increase cover prices at short notice. 22 Books reserves the right to show new retail prices on covers which may differ from those previously advertised in the books or elsewhere.

NAME ....

ADDRESS..

....

....

☐ I enclose my remittance for £_____
☐ I wish to pay by Access/Visa

Card number
☐☐☐☐ ☐☐☐☐ ☐☐☐☐ ☐☐☐☐

Card expiry date
☐☐ ☐☐

Please allow 28 days for delivery. Please tick box if you do not wish to receive any additional information ☐